Gently Used

Completely Made-Up Stories About Thrift Store Wedding Dresses

Advance Praise for Gently Used

"This book made me laugh so hard I cried, then cry so hard I laughed. At one point I had to sit down on a plastic chair near the donation bins and collect myself."

— A Stained Vera Wang, Goodwill, Aisle 3,

"Finally, a book that understands us. Especially the part about broken zippers and hope."

— Every Wedding Dress That Ended Up at Savers

"I stayed up all night reading this. My husband asked if I was okay. I said no and then kept reading. He slept on the couch. Worth it."

— Someone's Aunt Who Knows All the Best Thrift Stores and Will Tell You If You Ask

"Hilarious, heartbreaking, and hauntingly good. I am now ninety percent sure one of these dresses used to be mine. I need a moment."

— A Former Bride, Location Intentionally Withheld

"Henry and Helen's story wrecked me. I have not cried like that since my own wedding. Different reasons. Same mascara disaster."

— Anonymous Review, Five Stars, Still Emotional

Gently Used

Completely Made-Up Stories About Thrift Store Wedding Dresses

Nandi Sojourner Crosby

FREEDOM CONSCIOUS INK

For permission requests, contact the author at:

Nandi Sojourner Crosby, Ph.D.
Department of Sociology
California State University, Chico
Chico, CA 95929-0445

ISBN: 979-8-9885911-7-7

FreedomConscious Ink

This is a work of fiction. Names, characters, places, events, and incidents are either the product of the author's imagination or are used fictitiously. Any resemblance to actual persons, living or dead or to actual events or locales is entirely coincidental

CONTENT GUIDANCE

This collection contains stories dealing with terminal illness and death, grief and loss, fatphobia and body-based discrimination, family estrangement, and characters navigating asexuality/demisexuality. Brief references to workplace assault and bodily illness. All stories affirm LGBTQ+ identities and experiences.

"The dress only means something if you want it to. What is important are the people behind it. When it comes to these things that are handed down from generation to generation, each woman leaves her own mark on it, so that it tells our story, stitch by stitch."

—**Brenda Janowitz,** *The Grace Kelly Dress*

CONTENTS

For thrift store shoppers everywhere, especially the ones who know that second chances come with history, wrinkles, and occasional stains, and are more beautiful because of it.

ACKNOWLEDGMENTS

To my husband, LaMichael, the funniest person I know: thank you for laughing with me about us.

To Shuri, my cat, who sat on my laptop for approximately 50% of this book's creation: your contributions were significant, if not always helpful.

To Tracy, my best girlfriend, for helping me reimagine my own wedding dress when the custom, handmade gown I ordered from Etsy arrived from Ghana hot-glued and devastatingly disappointing. "No need crying about it," she said. And that's when I found a corset on Amazon and bought a feather neck cape from Temu that made me feel beautiful—despite a Tik-Toker calling me The Lion King after I shared my processional online.

This book is for anyone who's ever had to reimagine what beautiful means.

Author's Note

I have loved thrift stores for as long as I can remember. They have always felt like places where stories gather to catch their breath. Objects with pasts lean against objects still waiting for theirs, and if you walk slowly enough, if you let your fingers trail along the edges of things, you can feel it. That quiet hum. Lives brushing up against one another. Strangers who will never meet, connected by the weight of what they left behind.

But wedding dresses. Wedding dresses were always different.

Whenever I saw one hanging on a rack, pressed between a bridesmaid gown someone wore once and a blazer from 1998 that still smelled faintly of ambition and cigarette smoke, something in me stopped. Not paused. Stopped. Like recognizing a language you forgot you spoke. I would stand there studying it. Not just the style, though I noticed that too, the puffed sleeves or the Empire waist or the train that had given up halfway through its purpose. But the clues. The evidence. A stain shaped like a teardrop or a wine glass or regret. A hem frayed from dancing too hard, from spinning until the world blurred into joy. Pearls missing from the bodice like scattered prayers. A zipper that had clearly fought for its life and lost.

I always had theories. Wild ones that made me laugh out loud in empty aisles. Tender ones that caught in my throat. Funny ones I told at parties. Cynical ones I kept to myself.

I used to guess which former brides were now divorced based on the state of the dress. The ones pristine and flawlessly preserved, wrapped in plastic like museum pieces? Probably divorced within the year. Too careful. Too afraid of mess. The ones stained and ripped and stretched and loved? Those marriages tended to last longer in my imagination. I believed that the more a dress had lived, the more its marriage had too. That survival showed up in the fabric.

Decades ago, I started making up stories every time I found one. Stories about the bride who wore it, the family who witnessed it, the ceremony that blessed or cursed it, the secrets stitched into the seams. Stories about inheritances that felt like burdens and disappointments that felt like freedom and self-esteem measured in beadwork. Stories about the weight of expectation pressing down on tulle and the softness of second chances hiding in lace. I could look at a single bead pattern and imagine an entire household. A neckline could tell me whether the bride was bold or terrified or pretending to be both while her hands shook. A stain could reveal an emotional truth no one had meant to confess.

Sometimes, I giggled out loud at the stories I created in my head.

Eventually, I started buying the dresses.

The gorgeous ones that made my heart hurt. The tragic ones that looked like they had survived wars. The ones with more attitude than fabric, strutting even on wire hangers. The ones that shimmered like they had been through everything the world could throw at them and wanted to survive more.

I collected them until my closet threatened to file a formal complaint. Until I ran out of space and donated them right back to the store, completing the circle, so someone else could feel the tug I had felt. Because dresses that enter your life through a thrift store belong to everyone eventually. They are not meant to be kept. They are meant to keep moving.

Once, I posted a photo online of a rack of thrift store wedding dresses, all of them leaning together like exhausted dancers after the show. Within minutes, a colleague messaged me.

"That's my wedding dress," she said. "Third from the left."

Her dress had migrated from her closet to my camera to her memory, traveling through time and space to find her again. That is the magic of thrift stores. Everything returns. Everything reimagines itself. Everything carries a story, and sometimes those stories find their way back to the people who lived them.

This book was born from that magic.

These stories grew from a fascination with objects that outlive their moments, and from the stubborn belief that meaning does not evaporate just because circumstances change. That a thrift store wedding dress carries all its previous lives inside its seams the way we carry ours. Love and grief and ambition and pain, all folded together. The people we used to be and the people we wish we were and the people we are becoming despite everything. What was given to us and what we had to salvage on our own, with our own hands, making do with whatever thread we could find.

I wrote these stories because I wanted a place where humor and heartbreak could live side by side without apologizing to each other. Where identity and class and community and queerness and aging and culture and grief and joy and second chances could all show up to the same party wearing whatever they wanted. A place where a dress could hold a secret, a blessing, a memory, a lesson, or a punchline, and all of those things could be true at once. A place where the beautiful and the ridiculous both mattered, because they do. A place where the characters are stitched together not perfectly, but honestly, with crooked seams and loose threads and the occasional bloodstain from where the needle slipped.

I hope this book makes you laugh until you snort. I hope it makes you feel something you did not expect to feel today. I hope you find a story that feels familiar in the way an old dress feels familiar, even if you have never worn it, because you recognize the shape of the body that did. I hope it reminds you that life rarely moves in straight lines, that the best stories have stains, and that secondhand things often hold the richest truths.

Most of all, I hope you see yourself somewhere in these pages. Not the polished version you show the world. Not the bridal magazine version with perfect lighting and airbrushed joy. But the real one. The one who has survived something and carries the proof in her bones. The one who has outgrown something and left it behind like a dress that no longer fits. The one who has stitched herself back together again and again with whatever she had on hand—humor and grace and stubbornness and yes, a little thrift store magic.

Welcome to *Gently Used: Completely Made Up Stories of Thrift Store Wedding Dresses*.

May these stories shimmer for you. May they whisper truths you needed to hear. May they shine.

Where Her Heart Would Rest

Henry Goldberg was seventy-nine years old and still wore his wedding ring like it was fused to his soul.

People asked him once why he never took it off, not even after Helen died.

He'd shrugged and said, "Because she'll show up in my dreams and yell at me. You never met Helen. She could win an argument while chewing a sandwich."

This usually got a laugh, which was the point. Helen had taught him that grief was tolerable if you kept it funny.

What he didn't mention was the other thing she'd taught him: how to hide when your body was quitting.

The congestive heart failure had started eighteen months before Helen's diagnosis, a cruel irony that still made him want to shake his fist at whatever cosmic comedian was writing their story. His heart was slowly drowning itself, filling with fluid it couldn't pump efficiently, turning every breath into a negotiation.

He'd learned to pause mid-sentence and pretend he was thinking. To sit down and call it "resting his feet." To blame the swelling in his ankles on "these damn shoes" while his heart struggled to move blood uphill.

Helen had known, of course. Helen always knew.

"You're not fooling anyone," she'd said once, watching him catch his breath after climbing the stairs. "Especially not me."

"I'm fine."

"You're a liar. But you're my liar, so I'll allow it."

She'd died first anyway, which felt like cheating. He'd been the one with the failing heart, and she'd been the one who left.

Now he walked San Diego with the familiar squeak of his orthopedic shoes, slower than he used to, stopping more often than he'd admit. His hair defied gravity in ways that suggested either excellent genes or an ongoing dispute with physics. And everyone from Hillcrest to La Mesa whispered the same nickname when he wandered into their thrift stores.

The dress guy.

But nobody, not the clerks, not his neighbors, not even Virginia with the three wigs at the senior home, knew the full truth.

The dress wasn't just a dress.

It was Helen's last request.

And Henry had lost it.

Two months before she died, Helen sat in her recliner knitting what she claimed was a scarf but looked suspiciously like an ongoing hostage situation between yarn and ambition.

The chemo had taken her hair but not her hands. Not her humor. Not her ability to deliver a punchline while her body was actively betraying her.

She didn't pause her knitting when she said, "When I go, I don't want some clearance-rack urn sitting on a shelf collecting dust like a participation trophy."

Henry looked up from his crossword puzzle. "What do you want?"

"Wrap me in my wedding dress," she said, needles clicking like small bones. "That dress heard more of my jokes than most comedy club audiences. Let it hear my last one."

He'd set down his pencil. "You want to be cremated in your wedding dress?"

"Wrapped in it," she corrected. "After. The dress deserves to retire with me. We've been through a lot together."

Henry had laughed, even though his throat hurt. "You don't want something fancier? Something new?"

Helen had looked at him over her reading glasses with the expression she'd used when he'd suggested she might want to "take it easy" during her stand-up career.

"Henry. I married you. Clearly, I'm not into fancy."

That was how she told him, quiet, fierce, funny, what she wanted.

He'd kissed the top of her head, where her hair used to be, the skin warm and unfamiliar. "Okay, troublemaker. You and the dress. Final show."

"Standing ovation only," she'd said, and gone back to knitting.

The dress lived in his wallet first. A photo from 1972, creased soft from being touched too many times, the edges worn to velvet. Helen stood in front of their apartment in the dress she'd made herself, her hair piled on top of her head, her smile absolutely triumphant.

The dress was a masterpiece.

Empire waist that sat just below her bust, giving her a silhouette that was both classic and subversive. Bishop sleeves that ballooned at the shoulders and tapered at the wrists, dramatic without being costume-y. A scalloped collar that hovered along her collarbone with quiet authority. The bodice was covered in tiny geometric beadwork, little constellations of crystals she'd sewn on by hand over six months, each one catching light like captured laughter. And draped across her shoulders, a pale rose stole, soft as breath, making her look like she was about to headline a revolution.

She had worn that dress when they eloped at City Hall.

She had worn it when she performed stand-up in smoky bars where the audience was three drunk guys and a bartender who'd heard it all before.

She had worn it when she auditioned for Johnny Carson's talent scouts and made them laugh so hard one of them cried.

She used to say comedy required commitment, and nothing said commitment like sweating under stage lights in a full wedding gown while talking about her mother-in-law's brisket.

The dress had been her uniform. Her armor. Her statement.

And now it was lost.

It happened like this:

Trevor, their grandson, had been helping clean out Helen's closet three weeks after the funeral. He was twenty-six, well-meaning, and had the organizational skills of a caffeinated squirrel.

"Pop, there's so much stuff in here," he'd called out. "Half of it hasn't been touched in years."

Henry had been sitting in the living room, staring at Helen's chair, trying to remember how to exist without her in it. His ankles were swollen. His chest felt tight. He should have been supervising, but grief had made him careless.

"Just... donate what she wouldn't want anymore," he'd said, his voice hollow.

Trevor had taken that instruction and run with it. Literally. Three trips to Goodwill, one to Let's Do It Again Thrift & Consignment, and two to a massive donation bin in a mall parking lot.

By the time Henry realized what had happened, the dress was gone.

"I thought it was old," Trevor had said, his face pale with horror. "I didn't know it was important. Pop, I'm so sorry. I didn't know."

Henry had wanted to scream. To throw things. To demand Trevor drive to every donation center in California and tear through every rack until they found it.

Instead, he'd put his hand on his grandson's shoulder and said, "It's okay, bubeleh. You didn't know."

But it wasn't okay.

It would never be okay.

Because Helen was waiting, and Henry had promised.

Every morning, Henry kissed his fingertips and pressed them to his wedding ring.

"Alright, Helen," he'd say. "Let's go find your dress."

Then he'd take his morning pills, the ones that were supposed to help his heart pump stronger and his body release the fluid it kept hoarding, and he'd head to whatever thrift store was on that day's list.

He showed the photo to every clerk in San Diego County.

The reactions were different everywhere.

At the Goodwill on El Cajon Boulevard, a teenager with purple hair and three visible piercings had squinted at the photo and said, "Is it like… vintage vintage? Or vintage with trauma?"

"It's vintage with marriage," Henry had replied, leaning against a rack of coats because standing too long made him dizzy. "So yes. Trauma is involved."

The kid had laughed and promised to keep an eye out.

9

At a tiny consignment shop in North Park, two older women with improbable hair colors had taken one look at Helen's photo and clutched their hearts.

"This woman has presence," the one with magenta streaks said. Her name tag read PATSY.

"This woman has opinions," the one with electric pink tips added. Her name tag read GLORIA.

"This woman would approve of our hair," Patsy finished, nodding decisively.

They noticed Henry was breathing hard. Gloria brought him water and a chair without making a fuss about it, which he appreciated more than he could say.

Within a week, they'd formed what they called The Bridal Brigade, a trio of elderly investigators with the energy of caffeinated squirrels and absolutely no sense of personal boundaries.

They created a bulletin board in the back of the shop labeled OPERATION HELEN, complete with fabric swatches, hand-drawn sketches of the dress, a map of San Diego with thrift stores marked in red, and a suspect list that included "Trevor, for being careless."

But it was Ramon who became Henry's anchor.

Ramon managed the Hillcrest Goodwill with the fierce efficiency of someone who'd survived Catholic school, three older sisters, and Filipino family gatherings where everyone had opinions about your life choices and wasn't afraid to share them.

The first time Henry had walked in, sweating and pale after the three-block walk from where he'd parked, Ramon had taken one look at him and said, "Sit down before you fall down. When's the last time you ate?"

"This morning."

"That's not recent enough. Sit. Wait."

He'd disappeared into the back and returned with a Tupperware container of lumpia and rice, still warm, and a folding chair.

"My auntie made too much," Ramon said, which Henry suspected was a lie. "Eat. Then tell me why you look like you're about to keel over in my store."

Henry had eaten the lumpia. It was the best thing he'd tasted in months, the pastry crackling between his teeth, the filling savory and rich with garlic and green onions. And he'd told Ramon about the dress.

After that, Ramon set aside every cream-colored gown that came through donations. He greeted Henry every visit with either food or updates, sometimes both. And he watched Henry like a hawk, noting the days when his color was bad or his breathing was worse.

"Nothing yet," he'd call across the store. "But I saved you a croissant. Sit down and eat it. You look gray."

"I always look gray. I'm seventy-nine."

"You look grayer than usual. Sit."

One afternoon, about four weeks into the search, Ramon had asked, "Why does this dress matter so much? And don't give me the short version. I want the whole thing."

Henry had pulled out the photo, his hands trembling slightly. The tremor was new, a side effect of the medication or the heart itself giving up, he wasn't sure which.

"My wife wanted to be wrapped in it when she died," he'd said quietly. "It was her last wish. And I lost it. So I'm trying to... I'm trying to fix what I broke."

Ramon had been quiet for a long moment, studying the photo.

"She made this?" he'd asked.

"Every stitch."

"She looks like she could run the world in that dress."

"She tried," Henry said. "Came pretty close."

11

Ramon had handed the photo back carefully, as if it were made of something more fragile than paper. "We're going to find it. And if I find it first, you name your next grandchild after me."

"I already have grandchildren."

"Then rename them."

Six weeks after the search began, Henry's body made a decision without consulting him.

He was at the North Park consignment shop, going through a rack of white and cream dresses with Patsy, when his vision went sideways. The fluorescent lights stretched into long smears. His chest felt like someone was sitting on it.

"Henry?" Patsy's voice came from very far away. "Henry, you're white as a sheet."

He tried to answer, but his lungs wouldn't cooperate. He sat down hard on the floor between the racks, surrounded by other people's discarded wedding dreams, and thought: Not yet. I'm not done yet.

Gloria called 911. Patsy held his hand and told him he wasn't allowed to die in her store because it would be terrible for business.

"Think of Yelp," she said, her voice cracking. "One star. Man died here. Very inconvenient."

He'd laughed, or tried to. It came out as a wheeze.

At the hospital, they told him what he already knew. His heart was failing faster now. The fluid was building up despite the medications. They could adjust his treatment, buy him some time, but the trajectory was clear.

"How much time?" he'd asked.

The doctor, a young woman who looked like she should still be in college, had hesitated. "Weeks, probably. Maybe a month or two if you're lucky. But you need to stop pushing yourself. Your body can't handle the stress."

"I'm looking for my wife's wedding dress."

"Mr. Goldberg…"

12

"She asked me to wrap her in it. She died three months ago, and I still haven't kept my promise."

The doctor had looked at him, then sighed and said, "We can set you up with home hospice. Keep you comfortable while you... while you do what you need to do."

"I need to find the dress."

"I understand. But you're not going to be able to search for it yourself anymore. You need to let other people help."

The hospice bed arrived on a Tuesday.

They set it up in the living room, facing Helen's chair, because Henry refused to die in a bedroom where he couldn't see the place she used to sit.

Danielle, the hospice nurse, was kind and practical and didn't sugarcoat anything, which Henry appreciated. She showed him how to use the oxygen when he needed it, adjusted his medications, and listened when he told her about the dress.

"So you've got a whole search party out there?" she'd asked, checking his vitals.

"Ramon at the Goodwill. Patsy and Gloria at the consignment shop. My grandson Trevor, who feels so guilty he's basically become a full-time thrift store employee." Henry paused to catch his breath. Even talking exhausted him now. "They're looking. I just... I can't look anymore."

"That's hard."

"It's terrible." He closed his eyes. "She asked me for one thing. One last thing. And I can't even do it myself."

Danielle was quiet for a moment. Then she said, "What if more people knew? What if we spread the word beyond San Diego?"

Henry opened his eyes. "What do you mean?"

"Social media. Facebook. Instagram. People love these kinds of stories. A man searching for his wife's wedding dress so he can keep his last promise to her. That's the kind of thing that goes viral."

"I don't know what viral means. Is that bad?"

"It means lots of people see it. Thousands. Maybe more."

Henry thought about it. Thought about strangers knowing his business, knowing Helen's story, knowing he'd failed her.

Then he thought about Helen, waiting.

"Okay," he said. "Do it."

Trevor handled the campaign because he was young and understood how the internet worked, which was more than Henry could say.

Within forty-eight hours, Helen's dress had its own hashtag: #FindHelensLaughter.

The story spread fast. Local news picked it up on day one. By day two, it had reached Los Angeles. By day three, national morning shows were calling.

Henry watched it all from his hospice bed, oxygen tube in his nose, Helen's photo on the nightstand where he could see it when he turned his head.

"Pop, this is insane," Trevor said, scrolling through his phone with wide eyes. "We've got people in Arizona looking. New Mexico. Someone in Texas found a vintage shop with a dress from the seventies and they're sending photos."

"Is it Helen's?"

Trevor looked at the photo. "No. Wrong era. But they're looking. Strangers are looking for Grandma's dress."

Ramon called every day with updates. The Goodwill was getting dozens of calls, people wanting to help, wanting to know if the dress had been found.

"Not yet," Ramon would report. "But I've got half of California checking their donation bins. Your wife's dress is famous now, Henry."

"She'd hate that," Henry said, but he was smiling. "She always wanted to be famous for her comedy, not her wardrobe."

"Well, she's famous for both now. Also famous for marrying a stubborn man who won't let her go."

"Never," Henry said. "Not until I keep my promise."

On the fifth day, something shifted.

Victoria Vortex, a drag queen who performed at a club in Hillcrest and had been following the story, made a video that changed everything.

Trevor showed it to Henry on his phone, propping it up so Henry didn't have to hold it.

Victoria was in full makeup, gorgeous and fierce, looking directly into the camera.

"Okay, listen up," she said. "I've been following this story about Henry Goldberg and his wife Helen's wedding dress, and I need to say something. We've been looking for five days. Every thrift store in San Diego has been torn apart. Donation bins have been searched. eBay, Poshmark, Depop, all checked. And nothing."

She paused.

"Here's the thing. That dress might be gone. Someone might have bought it. It might have been damaged and thrown away. We don't know. And Henry is dying. Right now. He's in hospice and he doesn't have a lot of time."

Her voice softened.

"So here's my proposal. We can't find Helen's dress. But we can make her another one."

She held up a sketch, rough but recognizable. The empire waist. The bishop sleeves. The scalloped collar.

"I'm a seamstress. I make costumes for drag shows. And I know a hundred people who sew. What if we rebuilt Helen's dress from scratch? With donated fabric, donated time, donated love. What if we gave this man his promise back?"

She leaned closer to the camera.

15

"If you want to help, DM me. We've got maybe a week. Maybe less. Let's do this."

Trevor played the video three times because Henry kept asking to see it again.

"She wants to make a new dress?" he said finally, his voice thick.

"She wants to try. Lots of people want to try. Pop, look at the comments."

Trevor scrolled through. Hundreds of responses. People offering fabric, thread, beads, time. People saying they wanted to be part of something beautiful. People sharing their own stories of love and loss and promises kept and broken.

"Helen would call this ridiculous," Henry said.

"Is that a yes?"

Henry looked at the sketch Victoria had drawn. It wasn't perfect. The proportions were slightly off. But it was recognizable. It was Helen's vision, filtered through a stranger's hands.

"It's a yes," he said. "Tell her yes."

What happened next was impossible.

That's the only word for it. Impossible.

Victoria coordinated the effort like a general directing a very talented army. She broke down the original dress into components based on the 1972 photo, then posted assignments.

Within hours, volunteers had claimed every piece.

A woman in La Jolla donated cream-colored silk that was close to the original.

A retired seamstress in Chula Vista took the bishop sleeves.

A quilting group in Escondido claimed the beadwork, even though they had no idea how they'd get it done in time.

Ramon's auntie, the one who made the lumpia, volunteered to embroider the scalloped collar. "I don't know this man," she told Ramon. "But I know love when I hear about it."

Patsy and Gloria hunted down a pale rose stole at an estate sale in Oceanside, driving ninety minutes each way to get it.

People worked through the night. Strangers became collaborators. The internet, which Henry still didn't fully understand, became a sewing circle spanning three states.

Victoria sent Henry daily updates.

Day one: "We've got the silk. Someone in Phoenix is overnighting vintage crystals. This is actually happening."

Day two: "The sleeves are done. The quilting group has finished half the beadwork. I don't know how they're doing this."

Day three: "We hit a snag with the bodice. The original had a specific structure we couldn't figure out from the photo. But someone found a similar pattern from 1971 and we're back on track."

Day four: "Henry. It's almost done. I'm coming to show you tomorrow."

On day five, Victoria arrived at Henry's hospice bed carrying a garment bag.

She was in partial drag, full face but casual clothes, and she looked exhausted in the best possible way.

The room was full. Ramon had come, holding a Tupperware container because of course he had. Danielle the hospice nurse. Trevor, pale and quiet. Patsy and Gloria in their brightest wigs. A dozen others Henry barely knew but who'd somehow become part of this strange, beautiful conspiracy.

"Henry," Victoria said softly. "We didn't find Helen's dress."

Henry nodded. He'd known this was coming. The original was gone, swallowed by the vast churning machinery of donation and resale.

"But we found something else."

She unzipped the garment bag.

The dress inside glowed.

It wasn't identical to the original. Henry could see the differences immediately. The beadwork sat slightly lower on the bodice. The crystals were a different size. The hem was half an inch shorter.

But it was beautiful. It was Helen's vision, built by a hundred hands.

"Half of San Diego made this," Victoria said. "People we don't even know sent fabric and thread and encouragement. A woman in Phoenix shipped us crystals from her grandmother's collection. The quilting group in Escondido worked sixteen-hour days."

She laid the dress across Henry's lap.

The fabric was cool and smooth beneath his hands, smelling faintly of new thread and donated effort. He ran his trembling fingers over the beadwork, each crystal catching the too-bright hospice light, scattering small rainbows across the white walls.

"There's something else," Ramon said. He knelt beside the bed and turned the bodice inside out.

There, stitched carefully into the lining with red thread, was a small square of black cotton.

Henry recognized it immediately. One of Helen's comedy T-shirts. The one she'd worn when she performed at the Laugh Factory, back when she was still chasing the spotlight.

FUNNY WOMEN DON'T WAIT FOR PERMISSION.

"We found it in a donation bin at Goodwill," Danielle said. "Mixed in with some other clothes. We couldn't find the dress, but we found this. So we put it where her heart would rest."

Henry made a sound that wasn't quite a laugh and wasn't quite a sob. He pressed the fabric to his face and cried into it, his whole body shaking, the silk absorbing his grief like it had been waiting for this exact purpose.

The room was quiet except for his weeping.

Nobody tried to comfort him. Nobody said it would be okay. They just stood witness while a seventy-nine-year-old man held a dress made by strangers and mourned the woman he'd loved for fifty-three years.

That night, alone in his hospice bed, Henry talked to Helen.

"You should see this dress," he said to the dark room. "It's ridiculous. A drag queen organized it for you. Ramon's auntie did the collar. There are crystals from Arizona."

He could almost hear her response. *Of course it's ridiculous. That's what makes it perfect.*

"It's not your dress," he said gently. "It's a replica. You know that, right?"

So what?

"So what? Helen, I promised you. I promised I'd wrap you in your dress."

You promised you'd wrap me in love. That's what you're holding.

Henry looked down at the fabric, barely visible in the dim light. At the careful stitches. The donated crystals. The hours and hours of labor from people who owed him nothing.

That dress, Helen's voice continued in his memory, *was never about the fabric. It was about what it represented. I wore it on stage because it made me brave. I wore it at our wedding because it made me feel like myself. The shape of it, the weight of it, the ridiculous drama of it. That's what I wanted to go out wearing. That feeling.*

"And this?"

This has more love in it than the original ever did. The original was just me, alone in my apartment, stitching my hopes together. This one is a whole city stitching for you. For us. For a story they wanted to be part of.

Henry felt tears sliding down his cheeks, but they were different this time. Softer. Like release.

You kept your promise, Henry. Not the way you planned. But when has anything in our life gone the way we planned?

"You got cancer."

Not planned.

"I lost the dress."

Not planned.

"And now strangers have built you a new one out of kindness."

Definitely not planned. But better. So much better.

Henry laughed, a wet broken sound.

"I miss you so much."

I know. Come find me soon. I'll be the one heckling God.

"He doesn't stand a chance."

Nobody ever did.

Three days later, they gathered for Helen.

The memorial wasn't in a funeral home or a church. It was in the community room of the senior home, with folding chairs and string lights and absolutely no pretense.

Exactly how Helen would have wanted it.

The replica dress lay on a wooden table in the center of the room, glowing softly under the lights. The pale rose stole draped just so. The beading catching every shift in the air, scattering light like Helen herself had scattered laughter.

Henry had insisted on being there. They'd wheeled his hospice bed into the back of the room, propped him up with pillows, made sure he could see everything.

He was too weak to stand. Too weak to speak above a whisper.

But Trevor stood at the front, holding Helen's urn. He'd asked if he could deliver Henry's words, and Henry had agreed, because some promises can be kept through other people's voices.

"My grandfather wrote this for my grandmother," Trevor said, his voice shaking slightly. "He asked me to read it because he can't speak loud enough anymore. So this is Henry, talking to Helen."

He looked down at the handwritten note, then began.

"Helen Goldberg was the funniest person I ever met. And the meanest. And the kindest. Sometimes all in the same sentence."

A ripple of soft laughter.

"She asked me to wrap her in her wedding dress when she died. She said the dress had heard more of her jokes than most comedy club audiences and deserved to hear her last one."

Trevor's voice cracked. He took a breath and continued.

"We lost the original. My grandson donated it by accident, and despite the best efforts of half of San Diego, we never found it. For a while, I thought I'd failed her. Thought I'd broken my last promise."

He looked up at the dress on the table.

"But then these people, most of whom I barely knew, decided to build her a new one. They couldn't find her dress, so they made her another. With their own hands. Their own time. Their own love."

In the back of the room, Henry watched through tear-blurred eyes.

"Helen would have said that's ridiculous," Trevor read. "She would have said, 'Henry, who are these weirdos? Why do they care about our story?' And then she would have cried. Because that's who she was. Funny and tough on the outside, soft as butter underneath."

Trevor lifted the urn.

"So here we are, troublemaker. You wanted to go out wrapped in your dress. This one is made of donated fabric and secondhand crystals and the labor of people who wanted to be part of something beautiful. Just like your comedy was. Just like our marriage was."

He carefully laid the urn on the dress, nestling it into the folds of fabric.

"Go make God laugh, Helen. But not too hard. He's old."

Afterward, they wrapped the urn in the replica dress, exactly as Helen had asked.

Henry watched from his bed, this last gift, and felt something shift in his chest. Not pain this time. Something lighter. Permission to let go. Permission to follow.

Ramon came to his bedside, still holding the Tupperware he'd brought. "You okay, Henry?"

"I'm good," Henry said, his voice barely there. "I'm really good."

"You kept your promise."

"We kept our promise. All of us. The whole city."

He looked around the room at the strangers who'd become family, the neighbors who'd become co-conspirators, the thrift store clerks who'd become friends.

"Your grandmother would have loved this," he said to Trevor. "All these people. She would have done fifteen minutes of material on it."

"What would she have said?"

Henry thought about it.

"Probably something like, 'It took me dying to finally get a good audience.'"

Trevor laughed.

"That's pretty good."

"I learned from the best."

Henry died five days later.

It was quiet. His breath simply slowed, then stopped, like a song fading out.

Trevor found him in the morning, already gone, a small smile on his face. The photo of Helen on his nightstand. The replica dress folded in a box at the foot of his bed.

On the nightstand, next to the photo, was a note in Henry's shaky handwriting:

Kept my promise. Coming to find you. Save me a seat.

Helen's urn, still wrapped in the replica dress, had stayed at the foot of Henry's bed since the memorial. He'd wanted her close.

Now they buried them together. Henry's body and Helen's ashes, side by side in the same grave, the replica dress tucked around them both like a blanket. Like a final embrace. Like fifty-three years of marriage refusing to end just because their hearts had stopped.

The funeral was standing room only. Half of San Diego showed up. Ramon brought lumpia. Gloria and Patsy wore their brightest wigs. Victoria Vortex performed a eulogy in full drag that Helen would have loved and Henry would have pretended to be scandalized by.

The headstone read:

HENRY AND HELEN GOLDBERG

Together Again Still Arguing About Who Gets the Last Word

Hand Stitched

The pothole on 223rd and Avalon had developed a personality, and that personality was malicious.

Rabbit had watched it grow over three years from a modest divot into a full-fledged crater with aspirations. Uber drivers cursed it in seven languages. Teenagers launched skateboards across it with the reckless faith of people whose spines still had warranties. During the last election, a city councilman had posed beside it with a shovel, promised swift action, and then vanished like a magic trick performed by someone who'd never actually learned magic.

The pothole remained.

Every Saturday morning, Rabbit made this same drive home from Second Bloom Thrift & Resale with her weekly haul. During the week, she worked there four days sorting donations and steaming wrinkles from secondhand coats, mentally marking the best wedding dresses and tucking them aside in the back room. But store policy said employees couldn't buy on days they worked. So Saturday mornings, she showed up on her day off, employee discount card in hand, and claimed everything she'd set aside.

This morning's collection: three overstuffed black trash bags full of silk, satin, and endless lace.

Some of the dresses would become her own reconstructions, transformed in her garage studio into something new. Others, the plus-size gowns in excellent condition, she marked differently. A specific tag. A specific notation. She knew there were people out there, quiet networks she'd never met but recognized by their handwriting on other tags, doing the same work she was. Building small rebellions one dress at a time. She left breadcrumbs for them, and sometimes, months later, she'd see one of her marked dresses show up somewhere else, passed along, still circulating.

Now she just had to survive the pothole.

She eased her dented teal Corolla toward that crater like she was approaching a sleeping dragon she'd personally offended in a past life.

"Not today, Satan," she murmured, gripping the steering wheel with both hands. "I have zippers to fix and a bride coming at noon. You will not get my axle."

Her left hand, small and turned inward like a sleeping bird's wing, rested against the bottom of the steering wheel while her right hand guided the turn. She held her breath, crept forward at a speed that would have embarrassed a determined turtle, and survived the drop with only minimal violence to her suspension.

"That," she announced to no one, "is what prayer and regular alignment get you."

She patted the dashboard like it was a loyal horse that had carried her through battle.

The Corolla had 247,000 miles on it, a passenger seat held together with duct tape and optimism, and a check engine light that had been on so long Rabbit had started to think of it as decorative. She'd driven this car through every version of her life. Single motherhood. Bill collectors. The year she'd worked three jobs and still came up short. The morning she'd finally paid off the garage and cried in this exact parking spot.

The car had earned its retirement, but Rabbit couldn't afford to retire it, so they had an agreement: she'd keep it running, and it would keep running. So far, the arrangement held.

She parked in front of her beige house in Carson, a modest square of shelter she'd fought to keep for more than two decades. The front looked ordinary enough. Patch of struggling grass. Two rosebushes engaged in a slow-motion battle with the California sun. A screen door that squeaked like it was auditioning for a horror movie.

But the magic lived behind the side gate.

The garage.

From the outside, it was just an old wooden door with peeling paint and a handle that required specific jiggling. Inside, it was her kingdom. A universe of lace, satin, pearls, and second chances.

Rabbit unlocked the side entrance, put her shoulder against the door (it stuck in summer, swelled in winter, and required physical negotiation year-round), and stepped into the warm light of her creation.

Her studio greeted her like an exhale.

The air smelled like fabric softener, old wood, and the particular mustiness of vintage textiles that had been rescued and were now waiting for resurrection. A flat-screen TV she'd rescued from a curb mounted on the wall, currently paused on a movie she couldn't remember starting. Probably something with Denzel. She had a type. A mini fridge hummed in the corner with the steady determination of an appliance that refused to die out of spite.

Above her workspace, a gallery of framed art: brides from every culture in fabrics that sang with history.

A Nigerian bride glowing in gold and coral, wrapped in layers that could command a room. An Indian bride in crimson and gold so rich it looked like she was wearing fire. A Shinto bride embroidered with cranes in flight, each stitch a prayer. A Harlem Renaissance bride in silk sharp enough to cut through anybody's low expectations. A Mexican bride in a dress that looked like it weighed forty pounds and was worth every ounce.

The gallery was her North Star. A reminder that brides came in every shade, every shape, every story. That white dresses were a recent invention, and tradition was just peer pressure from dead people.

Beneath that gallery stood the heart of her work.

Racks overflowing with thrifted gowns in every shade of white and al-most-white and gave-up-on-white-entirely. Ivory, cream, champagne, blush, a tragic beige that someone had definitely thought was elegant in 1999. Piles of fabric draped over chairs like abandoned clouds. Plastic bins overflowing with rescued beads, ribbons, lace, and approximately nine hundred buttons she'd saved because you never knew.

Every single dress had come from a thrift store. Second Bloom, mostly, where she worked four days a week and got first pick of donations. But also the Goodwill, that one Salvation Army that smelled persistently of moth-balls, even fancy consignment shops in Manhattan Beach and LA where rich people donated gowns they'd worn once and decided weren't worth the closet space.

Rabbit transformed them all.

She took a plain satin sheath and added a patchwork train of different laces, each panel telling its own story. She cut apart three ugly bridesmaids dresses in dusty rose, mint, and lavender and reconstructed them into a sin-gle gown with strategic color blocking that looked like sunset. She harvested beadwork from one dress, sleeves from another, a stunning back panel from a third, and created something that had never existed before.

Her dresses were gorgeous. Unexpected. Completely unique.

People cried when they tried them on because they'd never seen anything like them. Because Rabbit had a gift for seeing what fabric wanted to become instead of what it had been.

It was chaos with purpose.

Rabbit loved it the way some people loved children or gardens or boats they couldn't afford to maintain.

She set down the three overstuffed black trash bags and rubbed her shoulder, the muscle protesting from carrying weight it no longer appreciated. The tape measure she kept draped there like a stole shifted slightly with the movement, the metal end tapping against her collarbone.

"This," she announced to the dresses, "is why I need a teenager in my life. One with manners and a driver's license and no opinions about my organizational system."

She opened the first bag and immediately regretted her life choices.

A wedding dress stared back at her with the confidence of someone who had made several catastrophic decisions and refused to apologize for any of them.

It was white. Technically. The way mayonnaise is technically a food.

But the sleeves. Dear God, the sleeves.

They were detachable. Enormous. Shaped like something between butterfly wings and weather balloons, covered in rhinestones that caught the light like a disco ball having a nervous breakdown. Someone had bedazzled these sleeves with the determination of a person who thought more was better and too much was just getting started.

"Ma'am," Rabbit said to the dress, "I respect your journey, but we need to have a conversation about boundaries."

She hung it on the Maybe If I'm Desperate rack.

The second bag offered a dress that appeared to have been crocheted entirely out of doilies. Not doily-inspired lace. Actual doilies. Like someone's grandmother had spent forty years making decorative circles for coffee tables and then, in a fit of ambition, decided to stitch them all together into a wedding gown.

It had probably taken hundreds of hours.

It looked like a tablecloth having an identity crisis.

"Bless your heart," Rabbit whispered, hanging it gently. "Somebody loved you very much and had absolutely no sense of proportion."

The third bag held a dress with a train so long it had its own zip code. Rabbit pulled it out and kept pulling. And pulling. The train unfurled across her studio floor like a beige silk highway to nowhere.

"How did you even walk in this?" she asked it. "Did you have a team of people? A dolly? A forklift?"

She held up the bodice. Decent boning. Good structure. Excellent beadwork along the neckline. If she cut off about twelve feet of train, harvested the beads, and gave the whole thing a purpose beyond making bridesmaids earn their friendship, she could work with this.

"You and me," she told the dress, "we're going to have a talk about reasonable expectations."

She caught her reflection in the full-length mirror propped against the wall. Purple dyed onto the tips of her hair, bright as a bruise, bright as a promise, caught the light. She'd been dyeing it this color for fifteen years now, ever since the first gray hairs appeared and she'd decided age didn't get to dictate her palette. The purple was her signature. Her flag. Her way of announcing herself before she spoke.

Against the violet, her brown skin glowed warm, the undertones catching gold from the studio lights. She adjusted the tape measure on her shoulder, smoothed her worn jeans, and turned back to the bags.

The next dress had beadwork so delicate she had to stop and just look at it for a moment. Tiny seed pearls arranged in patterns that looked like lace, each one hand-sewn with the patience Rabbit recognized because she possessed it herself. The thread was silk, nearly invisible, requiring good light and steady hands and hours of sitting perfectly still.

Somebody's auntie had poured love into this dress.

Somebody's auntie had sat under a good light with reading glasses and steady hands and stitched prayers into every bead.

"There you go," Rabbit whispered, hanging it carefully on a padded hanger. "Somebody saw you. Somebody loved you. Now somebody else will too."

Her phone buzzed on the worktable, vibrating against a coffee mug that said "I'm silently correcting your stitching."

She glanced at the screen out of habit.

Not Tamar.

It was never Tamar.

Day 387 of her daughter not calling. Rabbit had stopped counting around day 200, then started again around day 300 because apparently, she enjoyed her own suffering.

The text was from Kayla, one of her regular brides. All caps, three exclamation points, a string of emojis that would have given Rabbit's generation collective anxiety.

RABBIT!!! EMERGENCY!!! WEDDING IN 10 DAYS AND MY DRESS DOESNT FIT!!!

Rabbit sighed. Typed back with her right hand, her left resting against her thigh: *What happened?*

GAINED WEIGHT. STRESS EATING. CANT ZIP. HELP???

Come by this afternoon. Bring the dress. We'll fix it.

YOU'RE A LIFESAVER I LOVE YOU

You'll love me more when you see the bill, Rabbit typed, but she was smiling.

This was the work she loved. The emergency calls. The panic. The moment when a bride walked in looking like the world was ending and walked out looking like herself again.

31

She set the phone down and walked to her current project.

A modest, white-ish wedding dress hung on the dress form in the center of the studio. Someone had donated it to Second Bloom three weeks ago with a note pinned to the hanger: "Found this in my mother's attic. She never wore it. Too sad to keep."

The dress had been torn. Badly. A massive rip down the back seam, probably from being stored poorly, the fabric pulling apart where it had been folded for decades. The lace on one sleeve was mostly gone, unraveled to cobwebs. Two buttons missing. A stain on the hem that looked like rust or maybe old wine.

Rabbit had spent two weeks reconstructing it.

She'd hand-stitched the back seam with silk thread, reinforcing it with a hidden panel of cotton she'd harvested from another dress. She'd replaced the damaged lace with panels from three different vintage nightgowns, blending them so carefully you couldn't tell where one ended and another began. She'd sourced new buttons from her collection, slightly mismatched but intentionally so, giving the dress character. The stain wouldn't come out entirely, so she'd embraced it, adding strategic tea-dyeing to the whole hem to make it look deliberate, aged, loved.

Now the dress looked like something out of a Stevie Nicks fever dream. Romantic. Imperfect. Absolutely beautiful.

She ran her fingers over the sleeve, feeling the texture of the lace, the places where her stitches held broken things together.

This was her gift.

Not just sewing. Anyone could sew.

This was resurrection. Taking things the world had discarded and showing them they still had value. Still had purpose. Still deserved to be seen.

She'd been doing it her whole life, with one hand that moved differently than the world expected and a heart that refused to accept anyone else's definition of impossible.

Her mother, Diane, had not worried. She'd looked at her daughter's hand and said, "She's perfect."

And when the doctors suggested therapy, surgery, interventions, her mother had said, "She'll figure it out. Let her be."

So Rabbit figured it out.

She learned to hold fabric with her left hand braced against her body, using the natural curve of her palm to create tension. She learned to pin with her teeth when both hands were needed elsewhere. She learned that her left hand couldn't do everything her right hand could, but it could do things her right hand couldn't, like holding delicate fabric without crushing it, like creating gentle pressure that guided seams into alignment.

She learned that different wasn't broken.

Just different.

At noon, Kayla arrived with her dress in a garment bag and panic in her eyes.

"It won't zip," she said, before Rabbit could even say hello. "It won't zip and the wedding is in ten days, and my future mother-in-law already thinks I'm not good enough for her son and if I show up in a dress that doesn't fit she's going to have a field day."

"Breathe," Rabbit said, taking the garment bag. "We'll fix it."

"How? I gained like fifteen pounds. You can't just magic up more fabric."

"Watch me."

She unzipped the bag. The dress was lovely. Simple A-line, ivory satin, fitted bodice with a modest sweetheart neckline. It looked effortless but required a very specific body to pull off.

Kayla's body had changed. Hips wider. Waist thicker. Breasts larger. She looked healthy. Glowing. Alive.

The dress looked judgmental.

"Try it on," Rabbit said. "Let me see where we're working."

Kayla changed behind the curtain, emerging red-faced and frustrated. The dress zipped halfway, then stopped. The fabric pulled across her hips, gaping at the back.

"See?" Kayla's voice was thick. "It's hopeless."

"It's not hopeless," Rabbit said calmly. "It's just not the right dress for your body right now. But we can make it the right dress."

She walked around Kayla slowly, assessing. Pinning. Thinking.

"Here's what we're going to do," she said. "We're going to add panels. Side panels in a complementary fabric. Not ivory, something with depth. Maybe a soft blush or champagne. Something that looks intentional, like it was always part of the design."

"That'll work?"

"That'll work beautifully. You'll have more room, the dress will move better, and honestly? It'll look more interesting than it does now."

She pulled out a bolt of blush-colored silk from her stash. Held it up next to the ivory.

"This," she said. "This is what the dress wanted all along. It was just waiting for you to grow into it."

Kayla started crying.

"I'm sorry," she said, wiping her eyes. "I'm just so stressed and my mom keeps asking if I'm sure about this wedding and Jake's mom keeps making passive-aggressive comments about the flowers and I've been eating my feelings and now I can't even fit into my dress."

"Hey," Rabbit said gently. "Your body isn't the problem. The dress is the problem. And we fix problems here."

"You don't think I'm a mess?"

"I think you're a human being preparing for a massive life event while everyone around you has opinions about how you should do it. I think stress eating is a completely reasonable response. And I think this dress is going to be more beautiful with these panels than it ever was without them."

Kayla laughed through her tears. "How much is this going to cost?"

"For you? Two hundred. That includes labor, fabric, and the emotional support I just provided."

"That's so cheap."

"I know," Rabbit said. "I'm terrible at capitalism. Now go home, stop stressing, and come back in three days for a fitting."

After Kayla left, Rabbit laid out the dress and began measuring. The panels would need to be precise. Curved to follow the natural line of the body. Integrated seamlessly into the existing seams.

She worked through the afternoon, her hands moving in the rhythm she'd known since childhood. Cut. Pin. Stitch. Adjust.

The light changed outside her garage windows, shifting from bright afternoon to soft golden hour. She didn't notice. She was in the zone, the place where time stopped and all that existed was fabric and thread and the quiet satisfaction of making something right.

By evening, the panels were cut from thrift store wedding dresses and pinned. Tomorrow she'd sew them. The day after, she'd do a fitting. The day after that, final adjustments.

She stood back, looking at the dress on the form.

It looked better already. The blush panels added dimension, visual interest, and movement. It looked like a dress that understood bodies could change and that change was beautiful.

She received a call from an unknown number.

"My name is Denise. I got married six months ago. I wore a dress I bought from a thrift store. A gorgeous, cream colored, with lace. And there was a letter sewn into the hem."

Rabbit's heart stopped.

"The letter was from someone named Tamar," Denise continued. "It was about leaving. About choosing yourself. About being brave enough to walk away even when it hurts. And at the bottom, there was a note that said, 'If you find this, please call the number below. Tell my mother I'm okay.'"

Rabbit sat down.

"I tried calling," Denise said. "The number was disconnected. So I did some internet detective work. I found your name on some wedding dress forums. People talking about a seamstress in Carson who does reconstructions. I figured it might be you."

"It's me," Rabbit whispered.

"The letter was beautiful," Denise said. "I cried reading it. My wedding was... complicated. My family didn't approve. I almost didn't go through with it. But reading that letter, knowing someone else had chosen themselves and survived, it helped. It really helped."

"I'm glad," Rabbit said, and meant it.

"I wanted to tell you that Tamar sounds amazing. And that I hope you two find each other again."

"Thank you," Rabbit said. "That means more than you know."

"Should I keep the letter? Or do you want it back?"

Rabbit thought about it. About holding onto things versus letting them go. About letters that traveled through wedding dresses to find the people who needed them.

"Keep it," she said. "Pass the dress on when you're done with it. Let the letter keep traveling. Maybe someone else needs to read it."

"Okay," Denise said. "I will. Thank you, Rabbit."

After they hung up, Rabbit sat in her studio and cried.

Not sad tears. Not exactly happy tears.

Something in between. Relief. Grief. Hope. The complicated cocktail of emotions that came from knowing your daughter was alive and well and not speaking to you, but that her words were out there in the world helping people anyway.

At midnight, she heard her phone buzz.

She almost ignored it. She was exhausted. Her vision was blurring. She needed to sleep.

But something made her look.

A text from an unknown number.

Hi Mama. It's me. Can we talk?

Rabbit's hands shook so badly she almost dropped the phone.

She called the number.

Tamar answered on the first ring.

"Mama," she said, and her voice was the same, achingly familiar, with that slight rasp she'd had since childhood. "It's me. It's really me."

"Baby," Rabbit whispered. "Oh baby, I've missed you so much."

"I know," Tamar said. "I'm so sorry. I'm so, so sorry."

"Don't be sorry. Just talk to me. Tell me everything."

And Tamar did.

She'd been in Chicago for over a year now. Working at a bookstore. Taking classes at community college. Trying to figure out who she was when she wasn't defined by being Rabbit's daughter or by the expectations everyone had placed on her shoulders since childhood.

"I needed to leave," Tamar said, her voice steady even though Rabbit could hear the tears underneath. "Not because you were bad. But because I was disappearing. I was so busy being who everyone needed me to be that I forgot to figure out who I was."

"I know," Rabbit said. "I read your letter. The one you left."

"I meant every word," Tamar said. "But I also didn't mean it the way it sounded. I don't think your life was a waste. I don't think you sacrificed for nothing. I think you gave me everything and I wasn't ready to carry the weight of that gratitude. So I ran. But I needed to come back. Not physically. Not yet. But like this. On the phone. Talking. Being your daughter again without all the pressure of being perfect."

Tamar sobbed. "Denise called me. About the letter. About the dress."

"I know."

"Why did you put my letter in someone else's wedding dress?"

Rabbit thought about how to answer. Thought about truth and lies and all the complicated space between.

"Because what you wrote was important," she said finally. "About choosing yourself. About being brave enough to walk away. About second chances. I thought whoever wore that dress might need to hear it."

"But it was your only letter from me."

"I know," Rabbit said. "But maybe it needed to live in the world instead of in my drawer. Maybe someone else needed your words more than I did."

"Mama," Tamar whispered. "I read that letter I sent you. The one you kept. And I sound so young. So sure that I was right and you were wrong. So certain that your life was a cautionary tale instead of just... a life."

"You weren't wrong," Rabbit said.

"What?"

"You weren't wrong," Rabbit repeated. "I did disappear. I did work myself to bone for everyone else. I did say yes to everything except what I wanted." She paused. "I've been thinking about it for a year. Since I read your letter. And you were right to leave."

"Mama—"

"Let me finish," Rabbit said, and her voice was strong now. "You were right to leave because you saw something I couldn't see. You saw that I was drowning and calling it swimming. That I was alone and calling it strength. That I built a beautiful life with my hands and forgot to build a life I actually wanted to live."

She took a breath.

"But here's what I need you to know: I'm not sorry I worked hard. I'm not sorry I sacrificed. Because I got you. And you were worth every aching hand, every missed meal, every lonely night. You were worth all of it."

"Then why did I leave?" Tamar asked, her voice breaking.

"Because you're smarter than I was," Rabbit said. "Because you figured out at twenty-six what took me fifty years to learn. That you can love people without disappearing into them. That sacrifice doesn't have to mean erasure. That you're allowed to want things for yourself."

They were both crying now.

"I'm struggling," Tamar admitted. "I've moved three times. I lost my first job. I'm taking classes but I can barely afford them. I'm lonely. I don't have it figured out. I thought by now I'd have some big revelation about who I am and I'd call you and say 'Look, Mama, I found myself and it was worth it' but I don't know if it's worth it yet."

"It's worth it," Rabbit said fiercely. "Even if it takes ten more years. Even if you struggle the whole way. It's worth it because you're choosing you. Because you're not shrinking yourself for someone else's comfort. Because you're brave enough to not know who you are yet."

"I miss you," Tamar whispered.

"I miss you every single day," Rabbit said. "But I'm not angry. I'm not disappointed. I'm proud of you."

"How can you be proud of me? I ran away. I broke my promise to call. I left you alone."

"You didn't break your promise," Rabbit said. "You're calling now. It just took longer than either of us thought it would. And that's okay. Some promises take time."

They talked for an hour.

About Tamar's tiny apartment that smelled like curry from the restaurant downstairs. About her job at the bookstore and the regular customer who always asks for romance novels and then pretends they're for his girlfriend. About the community college classes she's taking and how she might want to be a teacher, or maybe a social worker, or maybe something else entirely.

About Chicago winters and how Tamar bought a coat at a thrift store that makes her look like a purple marshmallow but keeps her warm.

About loneliness and learning to be alone and how those are two different things.

About Rabbit's studio and the absurd dresses that come through and the brides who cry when they see themselves transformed.

About the pothole on 223rd that still refuses to be fixed.

39

About everything they'd missed.

About everything they'd get to rebuild.

"I'm coming home," Tamar said finally. "Not permanently. Not yet. But I want to see you. In person. I want to hug you and tell you I'm sorry and I love you and I'm still figuring it out."

"When?" Rabbit asked.

"Next month. I already requested the time off work."

"Okay," Rabbit whispered. "Okay. I'll be here."

"I know you will," Tamar said. "You're always there."

"That's my superpower," Rabbit said, smiling through tears.

"No," Tamar said. "Your superpower is making broken things beautiful. You've been doing it my whole life. With dresses. With people. With me."

"You're not broken, baby."

"No," Tamar agreed. "I'm just becoming. And you taught me that was okay."

When they finally hung up, Rabbit sat in her studio and let the silence settle around her like silk.

Then she stood, walked to her worktable, and looked at the dresses waiting for their next beginning. Thrifted gowns that had been worn, discarded, forgotten. Each one holding the potential to become something new.

She picked up her measuring tape, adjusted it on her shoulder. Reached for her scissors, her thread, her reading glasses that she kept losing and finding in increasingly strange places.

She looked at the dress form where the other dress had hung, now empty, waiting for whatever came next.

And she smiled.

"Alright, ladies," she said softly to the waiting gowns, her purple hair bright in the studio light, her left hand curved like a question that had learned to become its own answer. "Who's next?"

Because this was the work.

Taking broken things and making them whole.

Taking discarded things and making them precious.

Taking old stories and giving them new endings.

She'd been doing it her entire life, with one hand that moved differently than the world expected and a heart that refused to accept anyone else's definition of impossible.

And she wasn't done yet.

Not by a long shot.

The pothole on 223rd and Avalon would still be there next Saturday.

But so would she.

And her daughter was coming home.

And between all of them, Rabbit was betting on love.

Security Bride

Darlene Torres had been a security officer at Valley Fair Mall for eleven years, and she was very good at it.

She could spot a shoplifter from thirty yards. She knew which stores had the worst theft problems (Bath & Body Works, always Bath & Body Works, people lost their minds over candles). She could talk down an angry customer, redirect a lost child, and evacuate a store during a fire alarm without breaking a sweat. She was professional, competent, and respected by everyone she worked with.

She was also extremely careful about keeping her work life and her personal life in completely separate boxes.

At work, she was Officer Torres. Polite. Efficient. Unflappable. She wore her uniform as armor and her authority like a well-fitted jacket. She was the person people called when things went sideways.

At home, she was just Darlene. She watched British baking shows. She had strong opinions about which grocery store had the best produce section. She owned a cat named Senator Whiskers who had never been elected to anything but carried himself with political gravitas anyway.

The two versions of herself never overlapped, and Darlene liked it that way.

Until the wedding dress.

The wedding dress was Sybil's fault.

"You have to come to the Halloween party," Sybil had said over lunch two weeks earlier. "I'm not taking no for an answer."

"I don't do costumes," Darlene said.

"You don't do anything fun."

"I do plenty of fun things."

"Name one."

"I tried a new bakery last weekend."

"Darlene, that doesn't count."

"They had olive bread. It was very adventurous."

Sybil had given her a look. The look. The one that said *I love you, but you're killing me.*

"Come to the party," Sybil said. "Wear a costume. Be a person for one night instead of a uniform."

"I'm always a person."

"You know what I mean."

And Darlene did know. She knew that she'd spent eleven years being Officer Torres and somewhere along the way had forgotten how to be anyone else in public. She knew that her coworkers saw her as competent and reliable and had no idea that she could sing every word of "Bohemian Rhapsody" or that she cried during dog food commercials or that she had opinions about celebrity breakups that she only shared with Senator Whiskers.

"Fine," Darlene said. "I'll come to the party. But I'm not wearing anything slutty."

"I would never suggest you wear anything slutty."

"Or anything that requires body paint."

"Reasonable."

"Or anything involving a wig."

"You're making this very difficult."

"I'm making this achievable."

Which is how Darlene found herself at Treasures & Finds Thrift Store on a Saturday afternoon, looking for something ridiculous enough to qualify as a costume but practical enough that she wouldn't spend the whole party adjusting it.

The store smelled like dust and possibility, with undertones of old perfume and the particular mustiness that came from decades of donated fabric waiting for second chances. Overhead lights buzzed, casting everything in a slightly jaundiced glow. Darlene moved through the racks with the same systematic approach she used to clear the mall at closing time.

She rejected a witch costume (too obvious), a flapper dress (too much fringe), and something that might have been a sexy crayon (too many questions).

Then she saw the wedding dresses.

There were maybe fifteen of them, hanging in a corner like abandoned dreams. Most were cream or ivory, demure and forgettable. But one was different.

It was white. Aggressively white. White that hurt to look at directly, like staring into an LED bulb made of fabric. The sleeves were puffed to the point of requiring their own engineering degree, standing away from the bodice like they were attempting escape velocity. The skirt was layers upon layers of tulle, so much tulle that the dress seemed to occupy space in dimensions science hadn't discovered yet. And at the small of the back, a bow.

Not a bow. THE bow.

It was the size of a decorative throw pillow, constructed from the same white fabric, starched into submission, standing at attention like it had opinions about zoning laws.

Darlene stared at it.

A young woman with purple hair appeared beside her, arms full of vintage scarves that smelled faintly of lavender and ambition. Her name tag said RABBIT.

"That one's special," Rabbit said.

"That one's a fire hazard," Darlene replied.

"Those aren't mutually exclusive." Rabbit shifted the scarves to one arm and reached out to touch the sleeve, her left hand curving against the fabric in a way that looked both practiced and gentle. "This is quality construction. Probably late eighties, when people still knew how to make things that lasted. The boning is intact, the seams are French, and look at this." She turned the dress slightly to show the back. "Hand-stitched details on the train. Someone put real work into this."

"Someone put real work into making sure the bride couldn't fit through doorways."

Rabbit laughed. "It's not subtle."

"It's structural."

"Exactly. It makes a statement."

"What statement? 'I have terrible judgment and unlimited confidence'?"

"More like 'I'm here and you're going to deal with it.'" Rabbit looked at Darlene with a directness that made people either very uncomfortable or very honest. "You should try it on."

"I need a Halloween costume, not a wedding dress."

45

"This would be a perfect Halloween costume. You could go as a bride. Or a runaway bride. Or a divorced bride seeking revenge through the power of tulle and spite."

"That's oddly specific."

"I've been watching a lot of reality TV."

Darlene looked at the dress again. At the ridiculous sleeves. At the absurd bow. At the sheer audacity of it.

She thought about Sybil's party. About all the people who would be there in their carefully assembled costumes, all of them trying just hard enough to be clever without being too clever. She thought about showing up in something safe and forgettable.

Then she thought about showing up in this.

"How much?" she asked.

"Forty-five."

Darlene had a coupon. Twenty percent off. She'd gotten it last week when she'd bought a perfectly sensible set of dish towels and a lamp shaped like an owl.

Thirty-six dollars.

"I'll take it," she said.

"Excellent choice," Rabbit said. "What are you going as?"

Darlene smiled. "Divorced Barbie."

Sybil's Halloween party was exactly what Darlene had expected: too many appetizers, too much wine, and a playlist that kept alternating between "Monster Mash" and Stevie Nicks for reasons no one could explain.

Darlene had arrived at seven wearing the dress, and the reaction had been everything she'd hoped for.

Sybil had opened the door, looked at Darlene, and said, "Oh my God."

"Too much?"

"It's PERFECT. Get in here."

The party was in full swing. Sybil's living room was packed with people in various states of costume commitment. There was a halfhearted zombie, a very committed Beetlejuice, three different cats (one sexy, two regular), and someone dressed as a QR code which was either very clever or very lazy depending on how you looked at it.

Darlene walked in and the room noticed.

"Is that a real wedding dress?" someone asked.

"Thrift store," Darlene said. "Thirty-six dollars."

"It's incredible."

"It's ridiculous."

"Those aren't mutually exclusive."

For the first hour, Darlene had more fun than she'd had in months. She drank wine. She ate seven types of cheese. She explained her costume concept to at least twelve people and got laughs every time. She danced to "Thriller" and the tulle moved around her like she was inside a very enthusiastic cloud.

The sleeves made it impossible to hold a drink without looking like she was performing surgery, but she'd adapted. The bow kept getting caught on doorframes, but she'd learned to enter rooms sideways. The train dragged behind her collecting crumbs and cat hair, but that felt thematically appropriate for a divorced bride.

She was standing in the kitchen, eating a jalapeño popper and discussing the logistics of the bow with Sybil's friend Marcus when her phone rang.

Her work phone.

Her actual supervisor Marcus.

Darlene looked at the screen. Looked at Sybil. Looked down at the wedding dress.

"Don't answer it," Sybil said.

"I have to answer it."

"You're off duty."

"He wouldn't call if it wasn't important."

She answered. "Torres."

"Darlene, I need you to come in."

"Marcus, I'm at a party."

"I know, and I'm sorry, but Kenny called in sick and we just got word that Carter's is doing a surprise flash sale. It starts in thirty minutes. The parking lot is already backing up onto the highway."

"It's October 29th."

"I know."

"Flash sales are for Black Friday. In November."

"Tell that to Carter's marketing department. Look, I need someone I can trust, and you're the best I've got. Please."

Darlene looked down at the dress. At the puffed sleeves that had their own zip code. At the bow that was currently wedged against the refrigerator.

"I'm in a wedding dress," she said.

Silence.

"I'm sorry, what?"

"I'm wearing a wedding dress. It's a Halloween costume."

More silence.

"Darlene, I'm going to need you to repeat that."

"Wedding. Dress. Thrift store. Very large. Currently preventing me from using both arms simultaneously."

"Can you change?"

Darlene looked at Sybil, who was mouthing *SAY NO* with increasing urgency.

"Not quickly," Darlene said. "The zipper situation is… architectural."

Marcus made a sound that might have been a laugh or might have been the beginning of a stress migraine. "How bad is it?"

"There's a bow the size of a throw pillow and sleeves that have opinions."

"And you can't take it off?"

"Not without assistance and possibly scissors."

48

"Okay." Marcus took a breath. "Okay. Here's what we're going to do. You're going to come in. In the dress. You're going to help me manage this disaster. And we're going to never, ever speak of this again."

"Marcus—"

"Darlene, I've got two thousand people descending on this mall in twenty minutes and one security guard. I will take what I can get. Even if what I can get is you in a wedding dress."

"This is a terrible idea."

"Noted. See you in fifteen."

He hung up.

Darlene looked at Sybil. "I have to go to work."

"In the dress?"

"In the dress."

"This is the best thing that's ever happened to me."

"I'm so glad my professional humiliation brings you joy."

"Document everything," Sybil called after her. "I want photos."

Darlene arrived at the mall at 7:43 PM wearing a wedding dress and a sense of impending doom.

The parking lot was already chaos. Cars circling like sharks. Drivers honking with the fury of people who'd been personally victimized by the concept of limited parking. Someone had set up a folding chair in a handicapped spot to save it, which was both creative and definitely illegal.

She radioed Marcus. "I'm here."

"East entrance. I'll meet you."

She walked through the parking lot, the train of her dress dragging across the asphalt like a very judgmental ghost. A family of four stopped and stared. A teenager took a photo. Someone yelled, "Congratulations!" which she chose to ignore.

Marcus was waiting inside. He took one look at her and his face did something complicated.

"Don't," Darlene said.

"I wasn't going to say anything."

"Your face is saying plenty."

"My face is remaining professionally neutral."

"Your face is laughing at me internally."

"That too." He handed her a radio. "Okay. Here's the situation. Carter's sale starts in ten minutes. We're expecting somewhere between two and three thousand people. Most of the mall security is already stationed at Carter's entrance. I need you on roving patrol. Crowd control. Shoplifting prevention. General peacekeeping."

"In a wedding dress."

"In whatever you're wearing, yes."

"People are going to photograph me."

"Probably."

"This is going to end up on the internet."

"Almost certainly."

Darlene looked down at the dress. At the tulle that seemed determined to occupy all available space. At the sleeves that made her look like she was constantly surrendering.

"If I do this," she said, "you owe me."

"Name it."

"Christmas week. I get first pick of shifts."

"Done."

"And you never mention this again."

"I'm going to mention it constantly, but I'll pretend I'm not."

She adjusted the bow, which had slipped sideways and was now threatening to take out a decorative plant.

"Let's go," she said.

The next two hours were a masterclass in absurdist crisis management.

At 8:15, she broke up a fight between two women over a discounted Ninja blender. The tulle proved surprisingly effective at creating a physical barrier. The women were so confused by her appearance that they forgot what they were fighting about.

At 8:47, she confiscated a shopping cart full of clearance sweaters from a woman who'd been using her six-year-old as a lookout while she stuffed merchandise into trash bags. The bow got caught on the cart. The woman tried to run. Darlene, still attached to the cart via bow, was dragged approximately six feet before the woman gave up.

At 9:03, she responded to a Code Yellow in the food court (unattended child) and found a small boy crying under a table. She couldn't fit under the table because of the dress, so she had to negotiate with him from outside. She traded him a pretzel from the nearby vendor in exchange for him coming out. Worked like a charm.

At 9:28, she caught a shoplifter running out of Spencer's with approximately four hundred dollars worth of merchandise stuffed into a backpack.

The shoplifter was fast. Darlene was faster. Or would have been, if not for the dress.

She chased him through the food court, the train flying behind her like a cape designed by someone who'd never actually seen a superhero movie. The tulle snagged on a chair. She yanked it free. The shoplifter dodged around the pretzel stand. She followed, the bow catching on the edge of the counter and sending napkins flying.

"Stop!" she yelled, which was technically protocol but had never once actually worked.

He didn't stop.

She grabbed the train of her dress with both hands, lifted it like she was fording a river, and ran.

She was gaining on him. Ten feet. Eight feet. Six feet.

He tried to cut through the Sears housewares section. Bad move. Darlene knew this mall like she knew her own apartment. She knew the shortcut through the perfume aisle would get her to the other side of housewares faster.

She took the shortcut.

The dress, apparently, had other plans.

The train caught on a display of scented candles. The entire display tipped. Darlene didn't have time to stop. She jumped; the tulle flying around her like a particularly aggressive parachute, landed on the other side, and came face to face with the shoplifter who'd been forced to stop because a very large woman with a very full cart had blocked his path.

"Hi," Darlene said, breathing hard.

"What the hell," the shoplifter said.

"Security. Put the backpack down."

He looked at her dress. Looked at her face. Looked at the backpack.

Put it down.

"Thank you," Darlene said, pulling out her zip ties.

Behind her, someone was filming on their phone. Of course they were.

"This is going on TikTok," a teenager announced helpfully.

"Great," Darlene said, securing the shoplifter's wrists. "Make sure you tag the mall."

At 9:35, she was radioed about a situation in the parking lot.

"What kind of situation?" she asked.

"Uh." Marcus sounded stressed. "There's a peacock."

"I'm sorry, what?"

"A peacock. In the parking lot. Someone brought their emotional support peacock to the mall."

Darlene closed her eyes. "That's not a thing."

"Apparently it's a thing."

"Emotional support peacocks are not a thing, Marcus."

"I'm looking at one right now. It's named Clarence. The owner has paperwork."

"What kind of paperwork?"

"The kind printed off the internet that looks very official but probably isn't."

"Where are you?"

"North entrance. Near the fountain. The peacock is displaying."

"Displaying what?"

"Everything. All of it. It's very dramatic."

Darlene walked to the north entrance.

There was, indeed, a peacock.

It was magnificent and absolutely, categorically not supposed to be in a mall parking lot. The tail feathers fanned out in a display that was equal parts beautiful and aggressive. The bird stood approximately three feet tall, eyeing passersby with the disdain of someone who'd never been told no in their life. It was surrounded by a crowd of people taking photos.

Next to the peacock stood a woman in athleisure wear and the confidence that came from never having consequences for anything.

"Ma'am," Darlene said, approaching carefully. "You can't have a peacock here."

"Clarence is my emotional support animal," the woman said, not looking up from her phone where she was filming the bird. "I have a doctor's note."

"Emotional support animals are typically dogs. Or cats. Sometimes rabbits."

"The ADA doesn't specify species."

"The ADA also doesn't apply to peacocks in mall parking lots."

"Clarence is very well-behaved."

Clarence chose that exact moment to release a sound that could only be described as a cross between a car alarm and a demon being exorcised. Several people jumped. A child started crying. Someone's car alarm went off in sympathetic resonance.

"Very well-behaved," Darlene repeated flatly.

The woman had the grace to look embarrassed. "He's usually better with balloons."

"I need you to take Clarence and leave."

"This is discrimination."

"This is a mall, not a petting zoo. Take the bird home."

"I want to speak to your supervisor."

"My supervisor is the one who sent me out here. Take the bird home."

They had a staring contest. Darlene had broken up domestic disputes, she'd faced down drunk teenagers, she'd once convinced a man having a mental health crisis to leave Spencer's Gifts peacefully. She could outstare a woman with a peacock.

The woman blinked first.

"Fine," she said. "But I'm writing a review."

"You do that."

She left, Clarence trailing behind her with his tail feathers dragging across the tile like he was too important to carry his own train.

Darlene watched them go, the peacock's feathers catching the parking lot lights like a drag queen exiting stage left.

Her radio crackled. "Darlene, we've got a situation at—"

She turned the radio off.

She walked to the security office, locked herself in the bathroom, and looked at herself in the mirror.

The dress was destroyed. The train was torn, mud-stained from the parking lot and marked with what looked like a tire track. The tulle was flattened on one side, crushed from being dragged across multiple surfaces. There was a mysterious stain near the bodice that she sincerely hoped was pretzel cheese. The bow hung sideways like a drunk satellite, barely attached, held on by what appeared to be spite and one remaining thread.

Her makeup was gone, sweated off during the shoplifter chase. Her hair looked like it had been through a wind tunnel. There was a scratch on her arm from the candle display and her feet hurt in a way that suggested she'd walked several miles in dress shoes that were never meant for actual movement.

She looked ridiculous.

She looked like someone who'd survived something.

She looked like someone who'd shown up and done the work even when the circumstances were completely absurd.

She started laughing.

Not polite laughter. Not professional laughter. Real laughter, the kind that came from somewhere deep and surprised her with its intensity, bubbling up from her chest like champagne that had been shaken too long. She laughed until tears ran down her face, cutting clean tracks through whatever remained of her foundation. She laughed until her stomach hurt, until she had to sit down on the closed toilet lid because her legs wouldn't hold her.

She'd spent eleven years keeping her work life and personal life completely separate, and tonight they'd crashed together in the most spectacular way possible.

She'd been filmed. She'd been photographed. She'd been witnessed by hundreds of people at her most ridiculous.

And it felt amazing.

When she finally stopped laughing, she wiped her face, fixed the bow as much as was physically possible (which was not much), and went back to work.

By the time the mall closed at ten, Darlene had appeared in twenty-three TikTok videos, six Instagram stories, and one live-tweet thread titled "SECURITY BRIDE: A JOURNEY IN SEVENTEEN PARTS." Someone had made a compilation video of all her appearances set to "Going to the Chapel." Someone else had created a fan edit set to Beyoncé's "Single Ladies" that was somehow both respectful and completely unhinged.

Local news had picked it up. Channel Seven had called the mall asking for comment.

Marcus found her in the security office at closing, sitting at the desk with her feet propped up, still wearing the dress because taking it off required more energy than she currently possessed.

"You're internet famous," he said.

"I saw."

"Channel Seven wants to interview you."

"Absolutely not."

"Corporate called. They think it's good publicity."

"Marcus, I got into a standoff with a peacock and tripped a shoplifter with my train. That's not publicity. That's a liability lawsuit waiting to happen."

He sat down across from her. Looked at her for a long moment.

"You did good tonight," he said.

"I looked like an idiot."

"You looked like someone who showed up when we needed you. Even when it was ridiculous." He paused. "Even when you could have said no."

Darlene looked at him. At his kind, tired face. At the mall beyond the office window, finally quiet, the stores dark, the chaos settled into the peculiar stillness that comes after everyone has left and the cleaning crews haven't yet arrived.

"Yeah," she said. "I guess I did."

She drove home still wearing the dress.

It was too much effort to change, and honestly, she'd earned the right to wear it a little longer. She stopped at a red light and caught the driver in the next lane staring at her through his window, his face doing something between confusion and delight. She waved. They waved back, completely baffled.

At home, she fed Senator Whiskers, who took one look at the dress and meowed with what Darlene chose to interpret as respect.

"I know," Darlene said. "It's been a night."

She made tea. She sat on her couch, the tulle spreading around her like a very tired cloud. She pulled out her phone and, against her better judgment, looked at the videos.

There she was, breaking up the pretzel fight with the weary authority of someone who'd seen it all. There she was, chasing the shoplifter with her train flying behind her like a cape. There she was, facing down Clarence the emotional support peacock with the dignity of a person who refused to be intimidated by poultry.

The comments were mostly kind. Some were hilarious. Several were marriage proposals, which she ignored. A few were from coworkers who were clearly never going to let her live this down.

But one stood out.

"This woman showed up to work in a wedding dress on a random Wednesday and still did her job better than half the people I know in actual uniforms. That's what professionals look like."

Darlene read it twice.

Then she called Sybil.

"You're alive," Sybil said when she answered.

"Barely."

"I've been watching the videos. You're everywhere."

"I know."

"You tripped someone with your train."

"I'm aware."

"You're a legend."

"I'm a disaster."

"You're both. That's what makes it perfect." Sybil paused. "Are you okay?"

Darlene looked down at the dress. At the torn train. At the bow that had given up entirely and was now just hanging on through spite and one remaining thread.

"Yeah," she said. "I think I actually am."

"You should keep the dress."

"It's destroyed."

"So? It did its job."

Darlene smiled. "Yeah. I guess it did."

She hung up the dress in her closet that night, torn train and defeated bow and all. She looked at it for a long moment, this absurd thing that had somehow shown her something important.

For eleven years, she'd kept her work self and her real self in separate boxes. She'd been professional. Competent. Reliable. But always careful. Always controlled. Always making sure the two versions of herself never touched.

Tonight, they'd crashed together in the most ridiculous way possible.

And the world hadn't ended.

She'd been seen. Fully seen. In all her absurdity.

And she'd survived.

More than survived.

She'd shown up. She'd done the work. She'd been professional and ridiculous at the same time, and somehow, it had worked.

"Thank you," she said softly to the dress.

The dress, of course, didn't answer.

But somewhere, in a thrift store across town, Rabbit was uploading photos of new donations to the store's Instagram account. And in the background of one photo, barely visible, was a garment bag hanging on the special rack. The rack where she kept the pieces that were too good to just put on the floor. The pieces that had stories.

Inside that bag was another wedding dress. One that crackled when it moved. One that had been donated with the instruction to "make sure it finds someone who needs it."

Two dresses. Two women. Two completely different stories about what it meant to take up space.

Darlene Torres, security officer, internet legend, survivor of the Almost November Savings Spectacular, had learned that being seen wasn't dangerous.

It was just being alive.

And sometimes, being alive meant showing up to work in a wedding dress and doing your job anyway.

The videos would fade eventually. The comments would slow down. Life would return to normal.

But Darlene Torres would remember.

And the next time someone asked her to do something outside her comfort zone, to let her personal self and professional self-exist in the same space; to be seen in all her complexity and contradiction, she'd think about this night.

She'd think about the dress.

And she'd say yes.

Like a Princess

Six weeks after her wedding, Kelly Williams walked into Boo'Jee Cheap-skates with the very specific intention of buying a clear jar she could use to create a terrarium.

She was not looking for a wedding dress. She was not looking for anything with a past. She had learned, recently, that the present required enough management on its own.

The wedding had been small. Fifteen people at Stacy's parents' cabin, under a maple tree that dropped helicopters into everyone's drinks like tiny green blessings. Kelly had worn a cream pantsuit from Nordstrom Rack and Stacy had worn a sundress the color of peaches. They'd written their vows on index cards and Kelly's hands had shaken so badly the cards made a shuffling sound against each other, a soft percussion of nerves and hope.

"I promise," Kelly had read, "to love you exactly as you are, which is to say, perfectly."

Stacy had cried. Kelly's mother cried. Kelly's aunt Candace cried and then loudly announced that she'd "always known" even though she'd spent the first twenty-three years of Kelly's life using the wrong name and pronouns.

It was perfect.

It had also been terrifying.

Not the wedding itself. Not Stacy. But the aftermath. The part where Kelly woke up every morning in their apartment and thought, *This is real. This is my actual life. I get to have this.*

The part where she kept waiting for someone to notice she'd gotten away with something.

That was the pleasure of thrift stores, though. You entered with a list and left with a feeling. You came for nothing important and found something that insisted otherwise.

The dress announced itself before she touched it.

A soft crackle. A papery sound, faint but unmistakable, like fabric clearing its throat.

Kelly stopped.

She scanned the rack again, confused, until she saw it. Hanging slightly forward, as if it refused to be absorbed into anonymity. Sleeves ballooned and unapologetic. Pearls dulled by time, missing in places, leaving behind small open mouths of memory. The skirt held light in rigid vertical bands, shiny in a way that felt sincere rather than fashionable.

When she slid it free from the rack, it answered her.

Crunch.

Kelly laughed. Quietly. To herself.

"Oh," she said. "You're not subtle."

The dress smelled like cedar, dust, and something floral that had learned to wait its turn, maybe lavender or rose water long faded. It felt

61

heavy in her hands. Not just weight, but presence. The kind that made you stand differently without asking.

Gracie, tucked under Kelly's arm, wheezed and lifted her head. She sniffed. Sneezed. Attempted to lick a sleeve. The sleeve crackled in response. Gracie recoiled, offended, then coughed like she was registering a formal complaint with the Better Business Bureau.

"This dress is anxious," Kelly whispered, delighted. "You two are going to get along great."

Gracie sneezed again, this time with enough force to make her entire body vibrate. A woman browsing nearby glanced over, saw the ancient pug, and smiled with the specific sympathy reserved for people who love dying pets.

Kelly had adopted Gracie three years ago from a rescue that specialized in senior animals. "She's got maybe six months," the woman at the shelter had said. "A year if you're lucky."

That was thirty-seven months ago.

Gracie had outlived every veterinary prediction through what Kelly could only describe as spite. Pure, concentrated spite. She refused to die out of what seemed to be mostly stubbornness and a deep personal investment in wheezing dramatically at inappropriate moments.

A clerk drifted past, glanced at the gown, and nodded.

"That one's loud," she said. "Came in a while back. Adrian said the woman who donated it told her it wasn't meant for quiet people."

Kelly felt something bloom in her chest. Warm. Uninvited. Familiar.

"Adrian?"

"He works here sometimes. He's the one who took the donation." The clerk gestured at the dress. "He said whoever wore this before really loved it. You could tell by how it was cared for."

Kelly ran her fingers along the taffeta, feeling the texture, each fold of fabric stiff with memory and starch. Someone had loved this dress. Had chosen it. Had walked down some aisle somewhere, making noise with every step, refusing to be quiet about their joy.

She had seen dresses like this growing up. On television. On women who moved down aisles with certainty, all volume and confidence and futures that did not require explanation. She had watched them with a complicated wanting, a longing she didn't yet have words for. Not to marry those women. To *be* them. To wear a dress like that and have it mean what it was supposed to mean.

In eighth grade, standing in the tuxedo section of a rental shop before his cousin's wedding, Kelly had looked at the wedding dresses visible through the doorway and felt something break open inside. A recognition. A grief. A certainty that this, the dress, the bride, the woman, was meant to be hers. That somehow, she'd been given the wrong script, the wrong costume, the wrong life.

She'd buried it. The way you bury anything you know the world won't let you keep.

She'd tried being the boy everyone said she was. She'd dated girls in high school. Nice girls. Girls who held her hand at movies and kissed her goodnight and never understood why she always seemed distant, why she never quite met their eyes when they said her old name. She'd gone to prom with a girl named Rachel who'd looked beautiful in her dress and Kelly had spent the whole night feeling like she was watching herself from very far away, a stranger inhabiting her own body.

"Did you have fun?" Rachel had asked afterwards.

"It was fine," Kelly had said, and meant it. Everything was fine. She was fine.

Fine was the only safe answer.

She'd come out to her parents at twenty-five, sitting at their kitchen table, her prepared speech crumbling into, "I'm trans and I'm sorry."

Her father had looked up from his newspaper. "Why are you sorry?"

"Because I know this isn't what you wanted."

"Kelly," her mother had said gently, and it was the first time she'd used that name, the right name, and Kelly had started crying before her mother even finished the sentence. "We want you to be happy. That's all we've ever wanted."

Kelly had cried then. Not sad crying. Relief crying. The kind that comes when you've been holding your breath for so long you'd forgotten what oxygen felt like.

But even after coming out, even after transitioning, even after her parents' acceptance, which still felt like a miracle she hadn't earned, Kelly had moved carefully through the world. She didn't correct strangers who clocked her. She wore makeup that made her blend in rather than stand out. She'd learned to make herself smaller in a thousand tiny ways, each one so subtle she barely noticed she was doing it. Taking up less space in the subway. Softening her laugh. Apologizing when people bumped into her.

Until Stacy.

Stacy, who kissed her on the subway without checking if anyone was watching. Who called her "my wife" before they were even engaged. Who held her hand everywhere and didn't care who stared.

"You're so brave," Kelly had said once.

"I'm not brave," Stacy had replied. "I'm just tired of pretending. And you shouldn't have to pretend either."

Now, standing in a thrift store aisle, Kelly felt that wanting stretch its legs. The wanting that had been compressed for so long. The wanting to take up space. To make noise. To be seen.

The price tag read seventy-five dollars.

Kelly reached into her wallet and felt the corner of the coupon she'd been carrying for two months, stamped "Half Off Sunday" after she'd spent more than thirty dollars on a blender she didn't need and a glass vase shaped like a boot. She'd kept it without knowing why. A quiet faith in timing.

Thirty-seven fifty.

"Well," she said softly. "That feels like a sign."

Gracie wheezed her agreement, or possibly her objection. With Gracie, it was hard to tell.

The dressing room door stuck just enough to feel judgmental, the hinges protesting as Kelly pushed it open. Gracie curled into a loaf on the floor and launched into a coughing fit that sounded like a small engine trying to turn over. Kelly stepped into the dress, easing fabric over her hips, lifting the skirt carefully.

Crunch.

She froze. Then laughed.

"Okay," she whispered. "I hear you."

The zipper resisted, then gave in, like it respected persistence more than force. The sleeves rose around her shoulders, enormous and proud. The skirt settled noisily around her legs, the taffeta stiff and unapologetic.

She turned.

The mirror in the dressing room was old, slightly warped, the kind that made you look taller and stranger than you were. Kelly looked at herself in the wedding dress. Not her wedding dress. Someone else's. Someone who had walked down an aisle crackling like radio static, someone who had danced until they knocked over champagne glasses, someone who had refused to be quiet.

The bow stopped her.

Perfectly placed at her back. Gathering her in. Holding her shape like it had always known where it belonged.

She thought about being fourteen and trying on her mother's dress in secret, the afternoon when no one was home and the house was quiet enough to risk it. The way it had hung wrong, emphasized everything she was trying to hide, made her feel like an imposter playing dress-up in someone else's life.

This dress didn't hang wrong.

This dress fit.

Not just the measurements. The way it held her. The way it insisted she stand straighter. The way it made noise when she moved, refusing to let her disappear.

"I feel," Kelly said to her reflection, "like I should be processing this with a therapist. Or at least journaling."

The dress answered with a soft crackle, approving.

Gracie sneezed so violently she fell over sideways and had to struggle back into a sitting position. She looked personally victimized by the whole experience.

"You're being dramatic," Kelly told her.

Gracie wheezed indignantly.

Kelly turned again, watching the skirt move, listening to it announce her presence with every shift. She thought about Stacy. About their wedding. About the pantsuit she'd worn, cream-colored and sensible, an outfit that said "I'm just here, nothing to see."

She'd chosen it because it was practical. Because it didn't draw attention. Because it let her blend in.

She looked at the dress in the mirror. At the puffed sleeves. At the extravagant bow. At the way it crackled when she moved, announcing her presence whether she wanted to be announced or not.

She didn't know who had worn it before. She didn't know what it had witnessed. Only that it refused to disappear, and somehow, that felt important.

She bought the dress.

And the jar for the terrarium.

And another planter to house one of her hundreds of plants.

And an owl figurine that looked deeply concerned about something.

At home, Kelly hung the dress in their closet, tucked between Stacy's blazers and her own practical cardigans. It looked ridiculous there. Loud and proud and completely out of place.

Perfect.

Stacy came home an hour later to find Kelly sitting on their bed, staring at the closet.

"Why is there a wedding dress in our closet?" Stacy asked, dropping her messenger bag on the floor.

"I bought it."

"Why?"

Kelly pulled out her phone, scrolled for a moment, and handed it to Stacy. "Because of this."

On the screen, a woman in a wedding dress was breaking up a fight at a mall food court, her enormous tulle skirt billowing around her, her security jacket barely containing the puffed sleeves. The video was captioned "SECURITY BRIDE DOES NOT HAVE TIME FOR YOUR NONSENSE."

Stacy watched, her expression shifting from confused to delighted. "Wait, is this real?"

"She got called into work during a Halloween party. Didn't have time to change."

"And she just... showed up anyway?"

"And did her whole shift. There are like twenty videos. She tripped a shoplifter with her train."

Stacy scrolled through the compilation, laughing. "This is amazing."

"I know." Kelly took the phone back. "I saw it this afternoon and I just kept thinking about her. About how she could have said no. Could have gone home to change. Could have hidden. But she just... showed up. Exactly as she was. Making noise with every step."

Stacy looked at Kelly for a long moment. "And then you went and bought a dress that makes noise."

"I went and bought a dress that makes noise."

"I'm going to need more context."

Kelly stood and pulled the dress out. The hanger scraped along the rod. The taffeta crackled.

Crunch.

Stacy's eyebrows went up. "Oh."

"Right?"

"That's loud."

"I know."

Stacy reached out and touched the fabric. The dress responded immediately.

Crunch crunch.

Stacy laughed. Actually laughed, surprised and full and delighted. "Kelly. This dress sounds like you're smuggling chips."

"I know."

"Like you're wearing a bag of Sun Chips."

"I know!"

"The Sun Chips in the compostable bag that they had to discontinue because it was too loud."

Kelly was laughing now too. "Yes! Exactly like that!"

Stacy pulled the dress off the hanger and held it up, the fabric protesting with every movement. "Put it on."

"What? No."

"Kelly. You bought a dress that sounds like snack foods. The least you can do is model it."

"I already tried it on at the store."

"I wasn't there. Put it on."

So Kelly did.

She stepped into it there in their bedroom, Stacy helping with the zipper, both of them laughing as the dress crackled and protested and made its presence known. The sleeves puffed around Kelly's shoulders. The bow settled against her back. The whole thing announced itself with every movement.

Crunch crunch crunch.

Gracie, who had been napping on the bed, woke up and immediately began barking. Not her normal bark. Her special bark. The one that sounded like a squeaky toy being murdered.

"Gracie, it's just a dress," Kelly said.

Gracie was unconvinced. She barked again, lost her balance, and rolled off the bed with a thump. She landed on her feet, somehow, and continued barking from the floor with renewed intensity.

"Your dog is broken," Stacy said.

"Our dog," Kelly corrected.

"She's definitely yours right now."

Kelly spun. The dress crackled. Gracie's barking reached a fever pitch and then suddenly stopped as she ran out of air. She stood there, mouth open, no sound coming out, looking betrayed by her own respiratory system.

"Are you okay?" Kelly asked, concerned.

Gracie sneezed, coughed, and sat down heavily. She was fine. She was always fine. She would outlive them all through sheer spite.

Stacy was looking at Kelly with an expression Kelly couldn't quite read.

"What?" Kelly asked.

"You look beautiful."

"I look ridiculous."

"You look like yourself." Stacy stepped closer, adjusting one of the sleeves, her fingers gentle against the stiff fabric. "I've never seen you wear anything this loud before."

"I've never worn anything this loud before."

"I like it."

Kelly felt something crack open in her chest. Not breaking. Opening. "Yeah?"

"Yeah." Stacy kissed her, careful not to jostle the dress too much. "I like when you take up space."

"I'm working on it."

"I know you are."

They stood there in their bedroom, Kelly in a secondhand wedding dress that crackled like freedom, Stacy in her work clothes still smelling faintly of coffee and subway air, Gracie wheezing at their feet like a tiny asthmatic dragon guarding a hoard of medical bills.

"We should have gotten married in this," Kelly said.

"We can have another wedding," Stacy said. "We can have as many weddings as we want."

"Can we?"

"Kelly, we're married. We can do whatever we want."

And somehow, in that moment, Kelly believed her.

She wore the dress sometimes after that. Not often. Just when she needed the reminder that she was allowed to make noise. That taking up space wasn't selfish. That being seen wasn't dangerous.

She wore it when they hosted their first dinner party as a married couple and she introduced Stacy as "my wife" without hesitation, the words feeling less foreign in her mouth.

She wore it when they went to Pride and marched down Market Street with Gracie in a wagon decorated with rainbow streamers, the dress crackling with every step, announcing her joy to everyone whether they wanted to hear it or not.

She wore it on their first anniversary when Stacy surprised her with a cake and Kelly ugly-cried in their kitchen because she'd never expected to have this. To have someone who stayed. To have a life she didn't have to compress to fit into acceptable spaces.

She wore it to her first therapy session after the wedding, when her therapist asked how she was adjusting to married life and Kelly said, "I keep waiting for someone to take it away," and her therapist had said, gently, "What would happen if you stopped waiting and just lived it?"

The dress crackled with every movement. A constant reminder. A permission slip she gave herself, over and over.

You're allowed to be loud.

You're allowed to take up space.

You're allowed to be exactly who you are.

And somewhere, without knowing it, Kelly carried forward what the dress had witnessed before.

Not just one wedding. Multiple lives. Multiple women who'd needed permission to be seen.

A plus-size bride who'd worn it down an aisle and made everyone in attendance reconsider their assumptions about what beautiful looked like.

A security guard who'd done her job in it and learned that being ridiculous and professional weren't mutually exclusive.

A seamstress with purple hair who'd marked it as special and sent it forward to whoever needed it next.

Now Kelly. Learning that being quiet was not the same as being safe. That making noise was not the same as being rude. That taking up space was not the same as being selfish.

The dress remembered all of them.

And now it would remember her too.

To be loud.

To take up space.

To make a sound when she moved.

To walk into rooms crackling like her own personal percussion section, demanding to be noticed, refusing to shrink, finally, finally free.

Gently Used

SIX WEEKS LATER

Six weeks after her wedding, Tasha walked into Stuff & Things with the modest, hopeful intention of buying a ceramic planter shaped like a frog. She was not looking for her wedding dress. She was not looking for memory, irony, or the emotional equivalent of stepping on a rake in the dark.

That was the alchemy of thrift stores. A person entered carrying emptiness and left holding surprise. Came for nothing and walked out cradling a version of herself she had not planned to meet.

The store smelled like dust, artificial lemon, and donated fabric that had been stored in someone's garage for too long, breathing the scent of other people's finished chapters. Bright lights hummed overhead, casting everything in a jaundiced glow that made even new things look vintage, as if time itself pooled in the corners of this place and could not find the drain.

And then she saw it.

Hanging between a prom dress with a crooked corsage still pinned to its chest like a wilted prayer and a muumuu patterned with parrots frozen mid-squawk.

Her wedding dress.

Forty-five dollars.

A handwritten tag in blue ink declared, with casual authority: Gently Used.

Tasha did not gasp. She did not clutch her chest. She simply stopped, the way people do when time hiccups and the universe briefly forgets how to proceed. She knew the dress instantly. The specific shade of ivory that the Lulu's Outlet employee had called "champagne silk" while digging it from a bin of discontinued dresses. The beadwork across the bodice that caught light like scattered promises. The careful alterations she had begged for after losing weight too quickly on Ozempic and the specific anxiety that comes from planning a wedding while someone else's roommate treats boundaries like theoretical concepts.

The fabric felt thin under her fingers, the silk slightly rough from washing, the beadwork cool and smooth as river stones.

And then she saw the stain.

Small. Roughly the shape of Rhode Island. Nestled just below the waistline on the right side.

The mustard stain that Miles had created during the reception when he'd gestured too enthusiastically while holding a plate of German potato salad, launching a glob of jalapeño mustard onto her dress with the precision of a small catapult.

The stain that Eva had tried to clean before getting the dress professionally handled. The stain that had faded but persisted, visible if she knew

74

where to look, a small golden ghost that marked the exact moment joy had gotten messy.

Tasha exhaled slowly, the way people do when their thoughts scatter like marbles on linoleum. Then she took out her phone.

"Eva," she said when her best friend answered. "My wedding dress is at Stuff & Things."

There was a pause that contained multitudes. Then Eva said, with the precision of someone assembling a crime scene in her mind, "The one I was supposed to get dry cleaned?"

"Yes," Tasha said. "The very same. And it's forty-five dollars. With a handwritten tag that says 'Gently Used.'"

"Oh no."

"Oh yes."

"Lexi," Eva said flatly.

"I'm buying it," Tasha replied. "This is not a hostage situation."

"You should not have to buy back your own marriage."

"Well," Tasha said, eyes still fixed on the dress, "apparently I do."

A teenage employee chipped black nail polish drifted past. She glanced at Tasha. Glanced at the dress. Nodded once, solemnly, as if acknowledging grief in its natural environment. As if this store had seen everything and would continue seeing everything until the end of capitalism or the rapture, whichever came first.

The girl moved on, leaving Tasha alone with her matrimonial artifact.

SIX WEEKS EARLIER

Tasha had never expected to get married.

Before Miles, her dating life had been a long museum of misalignment. A gallery of almosts. Men who treated desire like a performance metric she kept failing to meet. Men who framed sex as reassurance she could never quite provide in sufficient quantity. Men who asked what was wrong with her, as if libido were a moral category with clear boundaries between virtue and deficiency.

The worst was Terrence. Three years of apologizing for her body's quiet refusals. Three years of him sighing like she had personally disappointed civilization. Three years of trying to want what she could not want, trying to manufacture desire the way other people seemed to produce it: easily, automatically, like breathing.

They ended things for the ninth and final time on a Tuesday. Tasha drove home and sat on her bed still wearing her jacket, her keys still in her hand, and stared at the wall for forty minutes. Then she opened her laptop.

At two in the morning, she found herself on Reddit in a forum called Dead Bedrooms. She had gone there expecting confirmation of her brokenness. The forum was full of high-libido partners mourning their sexless marriages, expressing rage and grief in equal measure.

She almost left.

But then she started typing.

[Dead Bedrooms] I think I'm the "problem" everyone here talks about

I'm the low libido partner. I'm the one you all vent about. And I don't know what to do anymore.

I've been with my boyfriend for three years and I can count on both hands the number of times I've actually wanted sex. Not the number of times we've had it (that number is much higher, because I love him and I try). But the number of times my body felt that pull, that want. It's so rare it feels like a glitch.

He says he feels rejected. He says it makes him feel unwanted. And I understand that. I do. But I also feel broken in a way I can't explain to him. Because I DO want him. I want to hold his hand. I want to fall asleep next to him. I want to cook dinner together and watch terrible movies and build a life.

I just don't want sex. Not the way he needs me to.

I've tried everything. Therapy. Hormones. Scheduling it like an appointment. Wearing lingerie that makes me feel like I'm performing in a play I didn't audition for. And every time, I feel like I'm failing some fundamental test of being human.

Everyone here talks about their HL (high libido) pain. And it's real. I see that. But nobody talks about what it feels like to be LL (low libido) and feel like you're fundamentally defective. Like your body is a betrayal. Like love should be enough to override biology but somehow it isn't.

I don't know what I'm asking for. Maybe just to be seen. Maybe just to know I'm not the only person who feels like this.

Maybe just to stop feeling like I'm broken.

The post sat there for eleven minutes before the first comment arrived.

You're not broken. You're just incompatible. Leave him.

Then another.

Have you had your thyroid checked?? Serious question, my cousin had the same thing and it was her thyroid the whole time.

Then one that landed like a fist: So you just lie there and make him feel like a rapist for wanting his own girlfriend. Cool. Really cool.

Tasha closed her laptop. Cried into her pillow. Decided she would never post again.

A week later, a message arrived from a stranger named Miles.

I felt every word of your post. I've never understood why people think closeness automatically means sex. Like there's only one way to build a life with someone. I'm on the asexual spectrum too. Demisexual, maybe? I don't even know the right words. But I know that what you described isn't brokenness. It's just being different. And different isn't wrong.

It was the gentlest sentence anyone had ever offered her.

They messaged for months. Long, winding conversations about everything and nothing. Books they loved. Meals they had ruined. Miles had a habit of sending voice memos instead of typing when he got excited, and his voice would climb half an octave when he was building toward a point, the words tumbling over each other like he was afraid the thought might escape before he finished explaining it. Tasha would listen to those memos two and three times, not always for the content, but for the sound of someone who had never once made her feel like she owed him anything.

And then, three months in, Miles sent a message at 2:47 in the morning.

I keep thinking about touch. Not sexual touch. Just... touch. The way my grandmother used to brush my hair back from my forehead when I was sick. The way my college roommate would lean his shoulder against mine when we studied late. The way closeness can exist without agenda.

I think that's what I've been looking for my whole life. Someone who understands that intimacy isn't a ladder you climb toward sex. It's just... intimacy. Its own complete thing.

Anyway. It's late. I'm rambling. But I wanted you to know that I think about the kind of relationship we could build. And it looks nothing like what other people expect. And that makes it perfect.

Tasha read that message seventeen times before she responded.

When can I meet you?

THE FIRST MEETING

They met at a coffee shop in Silver Lake on a Saturday afternoon when the light came through the windows like honey, thick and golden and slow.

Tasha arrived early, her stomach doing complicated gymnastics, her hands already shaking. She had picked a table near the back, somewhere she could see the door. Somewhere she could leave quickly if this turned out to be another person who would eventually ask her to be someone she was not.

Miles walked in at exactly 2:00 PM, and she knew him instantly. Not from photos. They had never exchanged photos. She knew him from the way he moved. Carefully. Like someone who had spent his whole life trying to take up as little space as possible. He had kind eyes and nervous hands and a T-shirt that said "Penguins: Nature's Formal Wear" in fading letters.

He saw her. Smiled. Walked over like he was approaching something precious that might startle.

"Tasha?"

"Miles."

"Hi."

"Hi."

They sat. Ordered coffee neither of them would drink. Talked for six hours straight. Miles had a way of listening that involved his whole body, leaning forward, going still, his coffee growing cold because he forgot it existed the moment she started talking. And when he spoke, he would press his thumbnail into the pad of his index finger, working through the thought physically, as if the idea needed to be felt before it could be said.

By the fourth hour, Tasha realized she had told him about Terrence. All of it. The sighing, the guilt, the three years of performing a desire she could not feel. She had not planned to say any of it, but Miles had a quality she could not name, a kind of patience that made honesty feel less expensive than it usually was.

It wasn't until the barista was wiping down tables with increasing aggression that Miles said, "Can I walk you to your car?"

Outside, the evening air was cool and smelled like jasmine from someone's garden, the scent drifting across the parking lot like a benediction. They walked slowly, neither wanting the afternoon to end.

At her car, Tasha turned to say goodbye, and Miles reached for her hand.

Not grabbing. Not pulling. Just reaching, his palm open, waiting.

She took it.

His hand was warm and slightly damp with nervousness, and he held hers like it was something rare. Not fragile. Rare. Something worth being careful with.

"I've been so scared," he said quietly, looking at their joined hands instead of her face. "My whole life, I've been scared that I was broken. That I wanted the wrong things."

He stopped. Pressed his thumbnail into his index finger. Looked up, his eyes bright with tears he was not bothering to hide.

"But standing here with you, holding your hand in a parking lot behind a coffee shop, I feel like I finally found someone who speaks my language."

She squeezed his hand.

"I spent three years apologizing to Terrence for not wanting him the right way," she said. "And now I'm holding your hand in a parking lot and it feels like the most intimate thing I've ever done. Not because it's leading somewhere. Because it's already here."

They stood there for a long moment, hands clasped, traffic humming in the distance, the jasmine scent thinning in the evening air.

"Can I see you again?" Miles asked.

"Yes."

"Tomorrow?"

"Yes."

He smiled, and it transformed his whole face, made him look like someone who had just been told he was allowed to stop holding his breath.

"I should warn you," he said. "I have IBS and it's embarrassing and loud. I burn eggs even though they're the easiest thing to cook. And I collect random animal facts and deploy them at the worst possible moments."

"I take up entire Sunday afternoons reading fanfiction about TV shows I don't even watch," Tasha said. "I'm anxious about everything. And sometimes I need to not be touched for days at a time."

"Perfect," Miles said.

"Perfect," she agreed.

He let go of her hand slowly, reluctantly, his fingers sliding away from hers like the tide retreating from shore.

She drove home with her hand still warm from his touch, still carrying the shape of his palm, and for the first time in years, she did not feel broken. She felt like she had been speaking a language no one else understood, and she had finally found someone fluent.

Within a year, she would try on forty-three dresses before finding the right one at a Lulu's Outlet, champagne silk with delicate beadwork, and she would think of that parking lot the whole time. The way his hand had felt. The way his voice had cracked on the word scared. She chose the dress that matched the feeling: something that looked simple until the light caught it.

THE MORNING OF

The morning of the wedding began gently, which should have been Tasha's first warning.

The wedding was small. Eva's backyard. String lights borrowed from a neighbor who had been promised they would be returned "at some point, definitely, we think." Folding chairs that had seen better decades. A buffet featuring German potato salad made by Miles's aunt, a woman who treated her potato salad credentials like a professional certification.

Inside Eva's house, surrounded by the particular chaos that comes from getting ready in someone else's bathroom, Tasha stood in front of the mirror wearing the dress.

It fit beautifully. Champagne silk that moved like water, catching light along the beaded bodice. The fabric was cool against her skin, slightly rough in texture, the kind of silk that felt expensive even though it had cost seventy-eight dollars on clearance.

Her makeup was soft, dewy, expensive-looking in a way that suggested professional intervention. Her hair was pinned just right, secured with approximately seventy-three bobby pins and the grim determination of a woman who refused to let humidity win.

Her pinky toe, however, was in active revolt.

"Eva," she said carefully, the way one might announce a small fire, "my pinky toenail is gone."

Eva looked up from her phone. "Gone how."

"Gone as in no longer affiliated with my body. Gone as in it has filed for independence and left no forwarding address."

Eva crossed the room and looked down. "Oh. Oh no."

"I know."

"How did this happen."

"I was shaving my legs in the shower this morning," Tasha said, with the hollow voice of someone recounting a preventable tragedy, "and I nicked my pinky toe. Just a tiny nick. I didn't even feel it at first. And then I looked down and there was blood. So much blood. Like, an alarming amount of blood for such a small area. And the toenail was just hanging there, attached by what I can only describe as a thread of pure audacity."

"Oh god."

"So I pulled it off."

"You pulled it off?"

"What was I supposed to do, Eva? Walk down the aisle with a half-attached toenail dangling like a tiny surrender flag? It was a mercy killing."

"Did you disinfect it?"

"I poured half a bottle of hydrogen peroxide on it and screamed into a towel."

Eva stared at her. "You can't walk down the aisle with an open wound on your foot."

"I bought closed-toe heels. Nobody will know."

"You'll know."

"I'll know a lot of things, Eva. I'll know that my centerpieces came from Five Below. I'll know that my neighbor is playing Gregorian chants at full volume because he thinks it helps his tomatoes grow. I'll know that Miles ate dairy at breakfast even though we've discussed this and his digestive system is about to file a formal complaint. I'll know many, many things. What's one more?"

Eva opened her mouth. Closed it. Opened a drawer and pulled out a small dropper bottle.

"What is that," Tasha asked.

"Serenity Drops. CBD and a little THC. Take two."

"Eva, I can't get high at my own wedding."

"You can and you will. Take the drops. Walk down the aisle. Every-thing will be beautiful."

Tasha took the drops.

THE CEREMONY

The ceremony happened on a Saturday afternoon in late September, and even the weather cooperated, which felt like a minor administrative miracle.

Tasha walked down the makeshift aisle barefoot.

She had planned to wear the heels. Had rehearsed walking in them twice that morning. But standing at the back gate of Eva's yard, looking at the twenty-three folding chairs and the string lights and the patch of grass where Miles was waiting, she kicked them off. The grass was cool and slightly damp beneath her feet, and her wounded pinky toe throbbed once in protest and then went quiet, as if even it understood this was not the moment.

The dress swished with each step. The beadwork caught the afternoon light, scattering tiny bright points across the silk like a constellation she was wearing. She could feel every thread of the fabric against her skin, the way it moved with her rather than against her, and she thought, absurdly, of the Lulu's Outlet employee pulling it from a bin, of that first moment she had seen it and known.

Miles stood at the end of the aisle wearing a suit he had bought at Men's Wearhouse and an expression she had never seen on his face before. Not his usual careful smile. Something wider and more unguarded, the kind of look people wear when they have stopped trying to arrange their face and are simply feeling everything at once. His hands were clasped in front of him, and she could see his thumbnail pressing into his index finger the way it always did when he was working through something big.

When she reached him, he took her hands in his, and she felt the same warmth as that parking lot in Silver Lake. The same careful tenderness. But now his hands were steady. Four years of learning each other had given him that.

"Hi," he whispered.

"Hi," she whispered back.

His eyes were already wet. She could feel her own throat tightening, the Serenity Drops doing nothing against the slow wave rising in her chest.

The officiant, Eva's uncle, a retired postal worker who had gotten ordained online specifically for this occasion, began speaking. Tasha heard maybe half of it. She was looking at Miles. At the small scar above his left eyebrow from a childhood bike accident he had told her about during their second month of messaging. At the way his jaw moved slightly when he was trying not to cry. At his hands holding hers with exactly the right pressure, the pressure that said I'm here without saying I need something from you.

She thought about the first time she had heard his voice, a rambling voice memo about octopus intelligence that had arrived at 11 PM on a Wednesday, his pitch climbing with excitement, the words tumbling and overlapping. She had listened to it three times and then pressed her phone against her chest like a teenager, like a person who had just been handed proof that the world contained more kindness than she had budgeted for.

Now he was standing in front of her, saying vows. His voice cracked on the word always. He pressed his thumbnail hard into her palm, and she pressed back.

When it was her turn, she said the words she had written at 4 AM the week before, sitting on the bathroom floor because she could not sleep. She did not remember all of them later. But she remembered saying, "I am not promising to be easy. I am promising to be honest. I am promising to stay." And she remembered the way Miles made a small sound, barely audible, that was not quite a laugh and not quite a sob but something in between that belonged only to him.

Eva cried. Mr. Chen next door turned up his Gregorian chants, perhaps sensing the moment needed spiritual accompaniment. Someone's phone buzzed loudly during the vows and was silenced with the urgency of a person defusing a bomb.

The kiss was sweet and brief and exactly right. Not a performance. Just a fact. A punctuation mark at the end of a sentence they had been building for four years.

They were married.

THE RECEPTION

The reception happened in stages, each one slightly more chaotic than the last.

The first disaster: the shoes.

Tasha had bought beautiful ivory heels. Christian Louboutin knockoffs from a website that promised "luxury for less" and delivered exactly that promise, with emphasis on the less. The red bottoms were spray-painted on, which she had known intellectually but had chosen to ignore because they looked perfect and cost forty-seven dollars.

She had put the heels back on for the reception, and what she had not anticipated was that spray paint flakes.

She discovered this approximately seventeen minutes in when she looked down and saw a trail of red flecks collecting beneath her feet and scattering behind her across the lawn, a dotted line marking everywhere she had stood and walked, like evidence at a crime scene.

"Miles," she said, grabbing his arm. "My shoes are molting."

He looked down. "Oh. Oh wow."

"I'm leaving a trail."

"Like Hansel and Gretel. But with shoe paint."

A beat passed. Then another. Miles bit his lip, waiting.

"That's not funny," Tasha said. But she was already pressing her mouth into a line, fighting it.

"It's a little funny."

She lost the fight. Laughed once, sharp and surprised, and then kicked the shoes off again, leaving her spray-painted heels under a folding chair where they could shed in peace. She walked barefoot across Eva's lawn for the second time that day, her wounded toe now collecting grass clippings like a tiny, horrifying souvenir.

The second disaster: the mustard.

Miles had been mid-sentence about emperor penguins ("Did you know they can dive to depths of over five hundred meters?") while holding a plate of his aunt's German potato salad, which was aggressive in both quantity and jalapeño mustard content.

He gestured. The plate tilted. Physics took over.

A glob of mustard landed on the dress with a wet splat that seemed to echo across the backyard.

Tasha looked down at the stain blooming against the champagne silk like a small golden continent.

Miles froze, plate still in hand, his face cycling through at least five emotions in rapid succession.

"I'm so sorry," he said.

"It's fine," Tasha said, and mostly meant it. The Serenity Drops had given her a kind of Buddhist acceptance of entropy. "It's just a dress."

But even as she said it, she knew that was not true. It was the dress she had chosen after forty-three others. The dress she had gotten altered three times. The dress that had reminded her of a parking lot in Silver Lake and the first person who ever held her hand like it was rare.

The dress that now had a mustard stain the approximate shape of Rhode Island.

"I'll get club soda," Eva said, already moving.

She dabbed at it immediately, her hands quick and efficient. The mustard faded but did not disappear. It left a ghost of itself, visible to anyone who knew where to look, a small golden shadow on the silk.

"I'll get it dry-cleaned," Eva promised. "Professional grade. It'll be perfect."

Tasha waved a hand. "It's just a dress."

Eva looked at her with the expression of someone who knew better but had the grace not to say so.

THE INTERRUPTION

The plan had been simple: Eva's roommate Lexi would stay out until morning.

Lexi was the sort of person who kept a gratitude journal and still managed to be thoughtlessly cruel, who would bring home flowers for the kitchen table and eat food she had not bought and genuinely not understand the difference. She had a way of filling a room that left no space for anyone else's plans.

She returned at 10 PM anyway.

Tasha was back in the dress for photos, still floating pleasantly on the last of the Serenity Drops, when Lexi walked through the side gate carrying opinions and a cup that smelled like crimes against coffee.

The conversation was brief, tense, and ended with Eva asking Lexi to leave in a voice that suggested this was not a request.

But the damage was done. The joy had been punctured, the way a single wrong note can silence an entire room.

Tasha changed out of the dress for the second time that night, hanging it carefully in Eva's guest room closet before leaving for the hotel Miles had booked as a surprise.

She was crying. Not dramatically. Just the quiet, tired crying of someone whose day had been interrupted by another person's bottomless inability to read a room.

The dress hung in the closet, champagne silk and beadwork and a small mustard stain, holding the shape of the day it had witnessed.

THE HOTEL ROOM

The hotel room was generic in the way all hotel rooms are generic. Beige walls. Abstract art that meant nothing. A bed with too many decorative pillows that served no earthly purpose.

But there were rose petals scattered across the comforter. Miles's attempt at romance, arranged by the front desk while they were at the reception, and the petals were already wilting slightly, curling at the edges the way real flowers do when they have been asked to perform for too long.

Miles sat on the edge of the bed, still in his suit pants and undershirt, his jacket lost somewhere, his tie unknotted and hanging loose. He was pressing his thumbnail into his index finger, the gesture Tasha now recognized as his body processing something his mouth had not figured out how to say.

Tasha stood by the window in the hotel bathrobe, her makeup half-removed, mascara smudged beneath her eyes.

"I'm sorry about Lexi," Miles said quietly.

"It's not your fault."

"I'm sorry about the mustard."

"Also not your fault." She turned from the window. "Well. Maybe a little your fault. Emperor penguins and potato salad are a dangerous combination."

He smiled, but the smile didn't hold. "I ruined your dress."

"You didn't ruin it. You marked it. There's a difference."

She crossed the room and sat beside him on the bed, rose petals crinkling beneath her weight. She took his hand, the same way she had taken it in that parking lot four years ago, and held it in both of hers.

For a long moment, neither of them spoke. His thumbnail was still pressing into his finger, even inside her grip. She pressed her thumb over his, stilling it.

"This day was chaos," she said. "My toenail fell off. My shoes shed evidence across the lawn. Lexi proved once again that she is a natural disaster in human form. And I got mildly high at my own wedding."

"When you list it like that, it sounds terrible."

"It was terrible. And also perfect."

"How can it be both?"

She turned his hand over in hers, traced the line across his palm. He went still the way he always did when she touched him with intention, not pulling closer, not asking for more, just receiving.

"Because at the end of all that chaos, I'm sitting in a hotel room with rose petals that are dying because you asked the front desk to scatter them and had no idea they'd wilt in two hours. And I'm holding your hand. The same hand."

Miles made a sound that was half laugh, half something else. He looked down at their hands.

"I was so scared today would be perfect," he said. "That everything would go right and I'd be the one to break it."

"Miles."

"And then I did. I threw mustard at your dress."

"Physics happened. And honestly?" She paused. "I'm glad."

He looked up.

"I'm glad the dress has evidence that today was real. Not some fantasy where everything goes according to plan and nobody's body does inconvenient things and love is just... effortless."

She moved closer, close enough that their knees touched, that she could feel the warmth of him beside her.

"Our love isn't effortless," she said. "We found each other in a Reddit forum at 2 AM because we were both too broken to sleep. We built this one message at a time."

"I know."

She rested her head on his shoulder. He rested his cheek against her hair. Outside the window, the city hummed its Saturday night hum: sirens and music and the distant protest of someone's car alarm. Inside the room, there was only the sound of their breathing, matched and steady.

He kissed the top of her head. Not a kiss that led somewhere. A kiss that said: This is where I am. This is where I'm staying.

After a while, Miles pulled back just enough to look at her.

"Want to watch terrible reality TV until we fall asleep?" he asked.

"More than anything."

They swept the rose petals onto the floor, changed into matching hotel robes, and climbed into bed. Miles found a marathon of a dating show so chaotic it made their wedding look like a masterclass in event planning. They watched three episodes, providing increasingly elaborate commentary, Tasha's bare feet tucked under his calf, her bandaged toe safely away from anything that could cause further injury.

She fell asleep with her head on his shoulder and his hand still holding hers.

When she woke up the next morning, the first thing she thought about was not the mustard stain or the shoes or any of the disasters. She thought about the way Miles had held her hand like it was rare. The way he had pressed his thumbnail against hers during the vows, a private language inside a public promise.

She thought about how, four years ago, she had been terrified that she was fundamentally broken.

And now she knew the truth: she had just been speaking a language no one else understood.

Until Miles.

SIX WEEKS PASS

Eva meant to get the dress dry-cleaned. She genuinely did. But life happened. Work happened. The dress hung in her guest room closet, the small mustard stain barely visible unless someone looked closely, and Eva kept meaning to deal with it but never quite found the time.

Until one Thursday morning when she came home from work and checked the guest room closet.

The dress was gone.

She found Lexi's note on the kitchen counter: Cleaned out the guest room. Donated some stuff. You're welcome.

The smiley face at the end of the note was, in Eva's estimation, a war crime.

Eva called Tasha immediately.

"I have something to tell you," Eva said. "And you're going to be upset."

BACK AT STUFF & THINGS

Tasha paid for the dress.

Forty-five dollars.

The teenage cashier rang it up without comment, as if women routinely bought back their own wedding dresses from thrift stores on random Tuesdays. The register beeped. A receipt curled out like a small white tongue.

Tasha carried the dress to her car, the garment bag rustling, the fabric inside still carrying the faint smell of Eva's guest room and the ghost of mustard and the specific loneliness of something precious left too long in someone else's closet.

She sat in the parking lot and held the bag in her lap.

The dress had held joy and nerves and vows and mistakes. It had survived mustard and spray-painted shoes and a roommate who kept a gratitude journal and still could not grasp the concept of other people's belongings. It had been worn during the happiest moment of her life and donated without permission by someone who understood neither boundaries nor the weight of champagne silk.

She called Miles.

"Hey," he said. "Did you find your planter?"

"I found my wedding dress."

Silence.

"At Stuff & Things. For forty-five dollars. With the mustard stain."

"Lexi?"

"Lexi."

A long exhale on the other end of the line. She could picture him pressing his thumbnail into his index finger, processing.

"Are you okay?" he asked.

"I'm sitting in a Stuff & Things parking lot holding my own wedding dress that I just purchased for the second time because Lexi has no concept of personal property and I married a man who cannot hold a plate near fabric. I don't have the emotional bandwidth for okay. I'm somewhere beyond okay. I'm in a different region entirely."

"I love you," he said.

"I know. I love you too. Even though you say 'no cap' wrong and apparently treat condiments like projectile weapons."

"Want to get Thai food tonight and watch terrible TV?"

"More than anything," she said.

And sitting there in the parking lot, she realized that was the truth of them. Not grand romantic gestures. Not passion that burned bright and fast. This. Thai food and terrible TV and a voice on the phone that climbed half an octave when it said I love you, the same way it climbed when talking about octopus intelligence or emperor penguins or anything else Miles found miraculous, which, it turned out, included her.

NOW

Now the dress hangs in their living room in a shadow box built by a man named Darryl who usually framed sports jerseys and had a lot of questions about the stain. "Is that mustard?" Darryl had asked, squinting through his bifocals. "Like, on purpose?" Tasha told him it was a design choice. Darryl did not look convinced but did not press the matter, which is all anyone can really ask of a framing professional.

The champagne silk has faded slightly, gone soft at the edges like old photographs. The beadwork still catches light, each crystal holding a tiny captured sun. The mustard stain is visible to anyone who knows where to look, a small golden ghost.

Sometimes, at parties, people see the shadow box and pause. A wedding dress, framed, in a living room. It invites questions.

Some guests think it is an art piece. Some assume it is ironic. A few have looked at Tasha and Miles, standing together in the kitchen, his hand resting on the counter beside hers without touching, and asked, with careful confusion, whether they are really married. Whether it is a real marriage. What they mean is something else. What they mean is that love which does not perform itself in the expected ways can be hard for other people to see.

The shadow box answers them without Tasha having to.

This happened. This is real. Look.

Tasha tells a different story about the dress every time someone asks. Sabotage. A curse. A roommate with poor boundaries. A penguin fact delivered at the wrong moment.

Only she and Miles know the whole truth.

The dress witnessed a wedding where the bride walked barefoot across damp grass because her spray-painted heels were shedding evidence and her pinky toenail had declared independence that morning in the shower. Where Serenity Drops made everything feel like it was happening at exactly the right speed. Where the groom loved penguins more than he loved coordination. Where joy got interrupted and still survived.

It witnessed a hotel room at midnight, rose petals wilting on a bedspread, two people holding hands and choosing each other not in spite of the mess but because of it.

Some marriages are built on passion. Some on faith. Theirs is built on comfort, shared humor, matching rhythms, and the mutual agreement that intimacy does not have to look like what everyone else insists it should look like. That love can be quiet and still be profound. That holding hands in parking lots is its own form of devotion.

Which, Tasha believes, is the rarest kind of love.

The kind that survives mustard.

The Handoff

Ruby Ridges had been doing Dolly Parton for so long that sometimes she forgot where the wig ended and her actual personality began. Fifteen years at The Cabaret, the same Friday night slot, the same opening joke about working 9 to 5 when she didn't wake up until 3 p.m. The audience still laughed. The tips still came. But lately, Ruby caught herself going through the motions like someone operating a vending machine: pushing the same buttons, dispensing the same product, wondering when the mechanism would finally jam.

The thing about doing Dolly, specifically, was that nobody ever questioned it. Dolly was universal. Dolly transcended. A Black drag queen from rural Georgia doing Dolly Parton was a crowd-pleaser, not a provocation, because Dolly herself had become so much bigger than country music that she barely registered as country anymore. She was sequins and sweetness and apolitical warmth, the safest possible version of white Southern womanhood, and Ruby had hidden inside that safety for a decade and a half.

She found the dress on a Tuesday, which was significant only because Tuesdays meant she had no reason to be wearing makeup or heels or anything that suggested she was more than a 38-year-old Black man with lower back pain and a Costco membership. Forever Finds wasn't even a planned stop. She'd ducked in to escape the Atlanta heat that pressed against skin like a wet towel, thinking she might browse the vintage leather jackets or silently judge other people's donated love stories.

Forever Finds was one of those sprawling thrift store operations that swallowed half a strip mall, a place where a taxidermied peacock could share shelf space with a bread maker and someone's entire wedding reception worth of centerpieces. The air conditioning wheezed with the effort of cooling so much square footage, creating pockets of cold and warmth that shifted as Ruby walked, like microclimates in a department store rainforest. This particular location was allegedly the largest in the Atlanta Metro area, and Ruby believed it. The formal wear section alone could have clothed every prom in Georgia, racks organized by color and occasion: quinceañera dresses in cotton candy pink and electric turquoise, bridesmaids' gowns in every shade of muted sorrow, evening wear that smelled faintly of mothballs and ambitious nights out. There was an entire international section featuring saris, kimonos, and what appeared to be a full Bavarian dirndl situation, which Ruby studied for a full thirty seconds before deciding she wasn't ready for that level of cultural adventure.

The wedding dress hung in the back corner, practically hidden behind a rack of bridesmaids' gowns in colors that God never intended. Prairie style, 1970s, cream-colored cotton with delicate lace panels running down the sleeves. Someone had reconstructed it carefully. The seams were straight, the hem even, the whole thing radiating a kind of stubborn dignity that made Ruby stop walking.

She touched the fabric. Soft. Substantial. Cotton that had been washed a hundred times and come out better for it. Nothing like the sparkle and synthetic shimmer she wrapped herself in every Friday night, fabrics that fought the body instead of moving with it.

Loretta Lynn had worn something like this on an album cover. Not the rhinestone Loretta of later years, but the young one, the coal miner's daughter who'd clawed her way out of Butcher Hollow with nothing but her voice and her nerve. Ruby's grandmother had loved Loretta Lynn with a devotion that bordered on religious. Mabel Ridges had cleaned houses for white families in Eatonton, Georgia, six days a week, and on Sundays she'd play Loretta records on a turntable that skipped on the loud notes, singing along while she braided Ruby's hair. Loretta sang about poverty and being looked down on and surviving men who didn't deserve the women who loved them, and Mabel would hum and say, "That woman knows," like she and Loretta were sharing the same testimony from opposite sides of a wall that neither of them had built.

Ruby had always wanted to do Loretta. Not a parody, not a campy wink, but a real tribute. Gritty, political, tender. Drag that made people think instead of just applaud. But a Black queen doing Loretta Lynn was a different proposition than a Black queen doing Dolly. Dolly was a theme park. Loretta was Appalachia, coal dust, food stamps, class resentment so specific it had a zip code. Ruby had heard the comments over the years, mostly from other performers, mostly said with a smile that didn't quite reach the eyes: "Country's not really your lane, is it?" As if lane were a neutral word. As if it didn't mean exactly what everyone in the room understood it to mean.

She'd never had the guts.

"That one's special," the cashier said. She was maybe twenty, with a septum piercing and the confidence that comes from not yet realizing the world can break a person. "Someone brought it in last week. Said it was reconstructed by some seamstress in California who only works with damaged dresses. Like, dresses with stories."

Ruby checked the price tag. Forty-two dollars. Reasonable. Terrifying.

She stood there holding the dress, feeling its weight settle in her hands like a question she wasn't ready to answer. She imagined herself in it. Imagined failing in it. Imagined the specific silence of an audience that didn't understand what they were looking at, a Black man in a reconstructed prairie wedding dress, lip-syncing Loretta Lynn in an Atlanta drag bar, and deciding it was either brilliant or a mess.

She put the dress back on the rack.

"I need to think about it," she said, already backing away.

The cashier shrugged. "It'll probably still be here. Not a lot of people shopping for prairie-style wedding dresses these days."

Ruby left before courage could catch up with cowardice.

She thought about the dress all week. Dreamed about it twice, which she found embarrassing. In one dream the dress was hanging in her grandmother's closet next to Mabel's Sunday dress, the navy blue one with the white collar that she wore to Greater Mount Zion Baptist every week without fail. In the other dream Ruby was wearing the prairie dress onstage, and the audience was entirely made up of Loretta Lynns, rows and rows of them, all nodding in approval.

She didn't go back.

Luna Tick showed up to The Cabaret three months ago with 47,000 Instagram followers, a reputation for viral TikTok dance challenges, and the dewy, unearned confidence that made Ruby simultaneously proud and exhausted. She was twenty-one, impossibly beautiful even out of drag, and possessed the particular fearlessness of someone who'd grown up with ring lights and algorithm optimization and had never had to learn drag in a world that wanted her dead for it.

She was also Ruby's drag daughter, which meant Ruby had taught her everything in the short months since Luna had walked into The Cabaret looking for a drag mother. How to tape. How to walk in six-inch heels on a beer-sticky floor. How to handle drunk bachelorette parties who wanted a person to be their gay best friend and their circus freak simultaneously. How to take a dollar bill without letting anyone touch what they hadn't paid for.

Out of drag, Luna Tick was Julio, a kid from Decatur who still lived with his mom and worked at Sephora, where he was, by his own account, "the best color-match specialist in the Southeast, and I am not being humble because humility is a scam." In drag, Luna Tick was six feet of Gen Z chaos and perfectly applied highlighter, all sharp cheekbones and TikTok choreography and the absolute certainty that the world owed her a spotlight.

That certainty was, if Ruby was honest, Luna's one genuinely annoying quality. Not because it was wrong, exactly, but because it was twenty-one in a way that made Ruby feel every single one of her thirty-eight years. Luna had opinions about everything. She had notes. She gave feedback that she framed as "just vibes" but that landed with the precision of a surgeon who'd watched too many YouTube tutorials on radical honesty.

Luna Tick showed up to The Cabaret every Friday night, even when she wasn't performing. She'd perch at the bar, long legs crossed, sipping something complicated with elderflower, watching Ruby's act with focused attention that felt less like judgment and more like devotion. Though with Luna, the line between the two was thinner than her eyeliner.

"That 'Coat of Many Colors' monologue really landed tonight," Luna said after Ruby's set one evening, materializing at her dressing table like a gorgeous, well-meaning ghost. "The audience was totally into it."

Ruby dabbed cold cream on her face, watching Luna's reflection in the mirror. The mirror was ringed with lights, half of which flickered, and it had witnessed fifteen years of Ruby's transformations and approximately three thousand pep talks Ruby had given herself before walking onstage. "Think it went long?"

"Maybe a tiny bit?" Luna perched on the counter, picking at her cuticles with a focus that suggested the cuticles had personally wronged her. "But like, in a good way. People love hearing the stories. The storytelling is really the best part of the act."

Ruby caught the implication and chose to let it pass. She peeled off her false eyelashes, the glue pulling at skin that was getting less forgiving every year. "Your set is at eleven. Should probably start getting ready."

"I've got time." Luna's voice went soft, careful, which was always a warning sign. "Ruby, can I ask something? And please don't get mad?"

Ruby's stomach dropped. Nothing good ever followed that sentence. "What?"

"Have you ever thought about trying something different? Not instead of Dolly, just in addition to? Because I genuinely think the range is there. I mean, clearly. I've seen it."

There it was. The gentle suggestion. The loving nudge. The implication that Ruby Ridges, fifteen-year veteran of The Cabaret's stage, might be getting stale. Delivered with the earnest compassion of a twenty-one-year-old who thought she'd invented the concept of artistic growth.

"I do other performers," Ruby said, keeping her voice even. "I did Patti LaBelle for Pride."

"That was three years ago."

"I did Tina Turner for New Year's."

"Ruby." Luna's voice was impossibly gentle. "That was the same year."

Ruby kept removing her makeup, her hands moving with the muscle memory of fifteen years, wiping foundation from her jawline, revealing the face underneath. The face that audiences never saw. The face that was just Darius, tired and thirty-eight and wondering when he'd become the kind of performer people described as "consistent."

"People come to see Dolly," Ruby said. "That's what they expect."

"I know. And the Dolly is legitimately the best tribute I've ever seen. I posted that clip of the 'Jolene' monologue and it got like twelve thousand views, which, for drag content that isn't a death drop, is insane." Luna hopped off the counter. "I just think there's so much more in there. But it's totally up to the artist. I'm just, the drag daughter. Contractually obligated to believe in the drag mother even when the drag mother doesn't."

She left before Ruby could respond, trailing perfume and good intentions, and Ruby sat staring at her half-cleaned face in the mirror, feeling something uncomfortably close to shame. It sat in her chest like a stone, not because Luna was wrong, but because Luna was twenty-one and had somehow already figured out the thing Ruby had spent fifteen years avoiding.

Bo had managed The Cabaret for seven years. She was a butch lesbian in her fifties who wore tailored suits from a Vietnamese tailor on Buford Highway, kept her salt-and-pepper hair cropped close, and carried the particular energy of someone who'd survived the Atlanta drag scene's roughest decades and lived to collect rent from it. She'd bounced at this same club in the early '90s, back when the parking lot was the most dangerous part of the evening. Now she owned the place, and she ran it with the efficient ruthlessness of someone who understood, in her bones, how quickly a good thing could disappear.

The Cabaret itself was a converted warehouse space on a side street in Midtown that had been a gay bar, a lesbian bar, a "mixed" bar, and briefly, during a confusing six months in 2003, a jazz club. The walls were painted black and covered with framed photos of every performer who'd ever headlined there, going back to the late '80s, faces in various states of glamour and defiance staring out from behind glass that nobody had cleaned since the Obama administration. The stage was a raised platform at the far end, flanked by speakers that buzzed if the bass got too heavy, with a lighting rig that Bo's nephew had installed and that occasionally dropped a gel filter onto a performer's head mid-number. The carpet, where it still existed, was the color of a bruise. There was a dressing room in the back with three mirrors, a communal counter permanently sticky with setting spray, and a mini-fridge that had contained the same bottle of Veuve Clicquot since 2019, waiting for an occasion nobody could agree on.

Bo called Ruby into her office the following Tuesday. The office was a converted storage room with a desk, a filing cabinet, and approximately forty years of The Cabaret's history crammed into manila folders that smelled like cigarette smoke and old leather. On the wall behind Bo's desk hung a framed photo of Sylvester, a framed photo of Bo's ex-wife (which Ruby had always found either deeply sentimental or mildly unhinged), and a handwritten sign that read: "This ain't a democracy. Tip accordingly."

"Sit down, baby," Bo said, gesturing to the folding chair across from her desk.

Ruby sat. Her heart was already going. Bo didn't do casual check-ins. Bo did announcements, verdicts, and the occasional threat delivered with maternal warmth.

"How long have I had Fridays?" Ruby asked, because she could feel what was coming the way a person feels weather changing.

Bo leaned back in her chair, which creaked like it was filing a grievance. "Fifteen years. And it's been good. Real good. Reliable. Professional. Audiences know what they're getting." She paused, and the pause was worse than anything she could have said. "But I'm making some schedule changes. Starting week after next."

"Changes."

"Luna Tick's taking Friday. I'm moving the Dolly show to Wednesdays and Saturdays."

The words landed in Ruby's chest like something heavy falling from a shelf. Fridays were prime real estate. Fridays were bachelorette parties and birthday groups with money to spend and phones ready to record. Saturdays were fine, a little more local, a little less electric. Wednesdays were the night people stayed home and watched television.

"Because she's younger," Ruby said, hating the bitterness in her own voice.

"Because she's different." Bo's voice wasn't unkind, but it wasn't sorry either. Bo had never been particularly talented at sorry. "Ruby, I love what I see on that stage. I love it. But I've loved the same version of it since 2010. People are mouthing along with the monologues. That's not evolution. That's a museum exhibit."

"So I'm being replaced."

"Refreshed."

"By my own drag daughter."

Bo was quiet for a moment. She picked up a pen from her desk, turned it over in her fingers, put it down. "I had a girl in the '90s. Velvet Rage. Lord, she could move. She did this Diana Ross number that made grown men weep. I'm talking actual tears, Ruby. Mascara on the bar napkins. And I told her, expand, try something new, because the audience was starting to thin out, and she said, 'This is who I am.' And I said, 'Fine.' And six months later she was doing that same Diana Ross number at a bar in Macon for twelve people and a bartender who was asleep."

Ruby felt heat climbing her face. "That's not the same."

"It is the same. It's exactly the same. And I'm telling this story because I didn't push hard enough with Velvet, and I've regretted it for twenty years." Bo stood up, the conversation clearly over, but she paused at the door. "Show me something new, Ruby. Anything. Show me the performer I know is in there. Because right now, I'm watching someone coast, and it breaks my heart."

Ruby walked out of Bo's office feeling like she'd been fired, even though technically she'd been rescheduled. The distinction didn't feel as meaningful as it should have.

She spent the next three days in a state of righteous misery. She rage-cleaned her apartment until the baseboards gleamed. She stress-ate an entire rotisserie chicken while watching RuPaul's Drag Race and delivering critiques to the television that were, she felt, more insightful than anything the actual judges were saying. She considered quitting. She considered doubling down, adding more rhinestones, making the Dolly act so extravagant it couldn't possibly be ignored.

On Thursday night, Luna texted.

Can we talk?

Ruby stared at the message for ten minutes. She cleaned the kitchen counter. She reorganized her wig heads. Then she typed back.

About what

I know you're mad. I'm sorry. Can I come over?

Fine

Julio showed up thirty minutes later, out of drag, wearing a hoodie and jeans and looking impossibly young. In boy mode, he was skinny and nervous, all knees and elbows and earnest brown eyes that hadn't yet learned the particular trick of concealing what they felt.

"I didn't ask for Friday," he said immediately, still standing in Ruby's doorway. "Bo didn't consult me. I found out from the schedule, same as everyone."

"But you're taking it."

"Yeah. I'm taking it." Julio walked past Ruby into the apartment, his movements uncertain, like he wasn't sure the floor would hold him. "Because I'm twenty-one and broke and trying to build something. But I didn't scheme. I didn't campaign. I just showed up and did my thing."

Ruby closed the door. "Well. Congratulations. Your thing is working."

"Don't do that." Julio turned to face her. "Don't be cold. I love this. I love what we have. The drag mother thing isn't just a title to me."

"Then what is it?"

"It's the reason I'm any good." His voice cracked slightly, and he looked away, embarrassed. Then he looked back, and there was something harder in his expression, something that was pure Luna Tick even without the makeup. "But I'm also not going to apologize for being talented. And I'm not going to pretend I don't see what's happening with the Dolly act."

"Nothing's happening with the Dolly act."

"Ruby. The bit about the coat of many colors? That monologue? That's the only part of the show where people stop looking at their phones. That's the part where the whole room goes quiet. And it's the part that isn't Dolly. It's the part that's actually something real."

Ruby felt tears threatening and hated herself for it. Crying in front of a twenty-one-year-old felt like a specific kind of failure she wasn't prepared to catalog.

Julio stepped closer. "You could have Friday back in a month if you wanted. All Bo said was try something new. Literally anything."

"I'm good at Dolly."

"You're incredible at Dolly. But is that all there is? The same jokes, the same stories, the same wig, forever?"

"It's worked for fifteen years."

"And it can keep working. On Wednesdays." Julio pulled out his phone, opened it, and showed Ruby a video. "Watch."

It was Ruby's performance from two weeks ago. The "Coat of Many Colors" monologue. Ruby watched herself tell the story of Dolly's childhood, the poverty and pride and a coat made from rags, and she watched the audience lean in, watched them actually listen, watched a woman in the second row put her hand over her mouth.

"See that?" Julio said softly. "That's when the act is really alive. That's when it's not a performance anymore. It's a conversation."

Ruby watched the video again. She did look different in that moment. More present. Less armored.

"I saw a dress," Ruby said quietly, surprising herself. "At Forever Finds. A couple weeks ago. Prairie style. Cotton and lace. Looked like something Loretta Lynn would have worn."

Julio's eyes went wide. "Loretta Lynn?"

"My grandmother used to play her records. Every Sunday." Ruby sat down on the couch, suddenly tired. "I've thought about doing a Loretta act for years. But Loretta's not Dolly. Dolly, everybody gets. A Black queen doing Dolly is fun. A Black queen doing Loretta Lynn..." She trailed off.

"Is political," Julio finished. "Is a statement."

"Is the kind of thing where half the audience doesn't know how to feel and the other half thinks I'm making fun of country music."

"Or," Julio said, sitting down next to her, "it's the kind of thing where people see a performer actually connecting to material that means something to her. Personally. For real." He paused. "Why didn't you buy the dress?"

"Because I'm a coward."

"You're not a coward. You're scared. Those are different things."

"Are they?"

"A coward doesn't dream about a dress for two weeks." Julio bumped her shoulder with his. "Go back and get it."

"It's probably gone."

"Then it's gone and the universe has spoken. But if it's still there..."

"Then the universe has also spoken?"

"Then the universe is doing everything short of writing it in the sky."

Ruby didn't go back the next day. Or the day after that. She went on Saturday afternoon, five days later, telling herself she was just going to browse, maybe look at the leather jackets, maybe see if the dirndl situation was still available, absolutely not thinking about a cream-colored prairie dress that she'd touched once and couldn't stop remembering.

Forever Finds was quieter on Saturdays, the fluorescent lights humming their same tired tune, the air conditioning still losing its battle with the Georgia heat. Ruby walked past the housewares section, past the books (seven copies of The Da Vinci Code, which felt like a sociological statement), past the shoe section where a woman was trying on roller skates with the focused determination of someone making a life-altering decision.

The bridesmaids' rack was still there, still ugly, still blocking the back corner. Ruby moved the hangers aside, their metal scraping and squeaking against the rod, and felt her breath catch.

The dress was still there.

It hung exactly where she'd left it, patient and undisturbed, as if two weeks hadn't passed. The cream cotton. The lace panels. The reconstructed seams, straight and even, holding together something that had once been damaged.

Ruby took it off the rack and held it against herself. In the smudged mirror propped against the wall, she could see the shape of it, the way it fell, simple and honest and nothing like anything she'd ever performed in.

The same cashier was working. She looked up, recognized Ruby, and smiled. "It waited."

"I see that."

"You want to try it on? Fitting room's open."

Ruby almost said no. Almost put the dress back for the second time. But she thought about Bo's office and the creaking chair and the story about Velvet Rage doing Diana Ross in Macon for twelve people. She thought about Julio showing her the video of her own performance, the moment where the act became real. She thought about her grandmother's turntable, the one that skipped on the loud notes, and Mabel's voice humming along with Loretta while she braided Ruby's hair with hands that smelled like Pine-Sol and cocoa butter.

"Yeah," Ruby said. "I'll try it on."

The fitting room was a curtained-off corner with a full-length mirror that had a crack running through the upper left corner like a lightning bolt. The fluorescent light was unforgiving in the way that only thrift store fluorescent lights can be, revealing every pore, every shadow, every truth a person might be trying to avoid.

Ruby put on the dress.

It fit. Not perfectly, not like it was made for her, but close. Close enough that the imperfection felt honest rather than wrong. The cotton was soft against her skin, nothing like the stiff synthetic fabrics of her performance gowns. The lace panels felt delicate, almost vulnerable. The whole thing made her look smaller somehow. Less like a spectacle and more like a person.

She stared at herself in the cracked mirror.

She looked like her grandmother. Not literally, not in the features, but in the bearing. In the way the dress suggested a woman who worked hard and didn't complain about it and found beauty where she could. Mabel Ridges, who had died before Ruby came out, who had never seen a single performance, who had never gotten to learn that the grandchild she'd raised had turned out brave enough to stand on a stage in front of strangers and be someone extraordinary. Or at least someone extraordinary at one specific thing.

Ruby bought the dress. Forty-two dollars. The cashier folded it into a garment bag with the careful attention of someone who understood that certain purchases are not really purchases at all.

She carried it to her car and sat in the parking lot for ten minutes, the garment bag draped across the passenger seat like a guest she'd finally invited.

That weekend, alone in her apartment with the curtains closed, Ruby put the dress on again and opened her laptop. She downloaded "Coal Miner's Daughter." She practiced the lyrics, stumbling over words she'd heard a thousand times as a child but had never tried to sing. She worked on her Loretta Lynn accent, which was closer to her actual voice than Dolly's exaggerated Tennessee drawl had ever been. Loretta's voice lived somewhere in the chest, in the throat, rough and unpolished, and Ruby found that when she stopped trying to perform it, it came out sounding almost like her grandmother's singing voice, that low, tired, beautiful hum that had been the soundtrack of every Sunday in Eatonton.

She practiced in front of her mirror every night that week. Some nights it felt real. Other nights it felt like a forty-two-dollar mistake. She kept going.

On Friday, she called Luna Tick.

"I need a favor," Ruby said. "I need a body in the front row when I debut the new act. Someone who'll clap even if it's terrible."

There was a pause. "You're really doing it?"

"I'm terrified. But yeah."

"Ruby." Luna's voice went thick, and Ruby could hear the shift, the raw thing underneath the performer. "When?"

"Friday after next. My first Wednesday slot. I want to debut it there, not Saturday. Smaller crowd. Lower stakes."

"That's smart. That's really smart." Another pause. "What are you doing? Which performer?"

"Loretta Lynn."

The silence that followed was different from the others. Ruby could feel Julio thinking, could feel the gears turning as he processed what it meant for a Black drag queen to choose Loretta Lynn in a city that was simultaneously the queer capital of the South and a place where Confederate flags still flew thirty minutes outside the perimeter.

"Oh," Julio said finally. "Oh, Ruby. That's going to be incredible."

"Or a disaster."

"Those are sometimes the same thing."

They met for lunch on Wednesday at a diner in East Atlanta, the kind of place where the booths had been reupholstered so many times that the seats felt like geological strata, layers of vinyl recording decades of spilled coffee and Sunday hangovers. The wallpaper featured a rooster pattern that someone had chosen on purpose, presumably during a period of personal crisis. Luna arrived in full face because she never missed a content opportunity, her makeup flawless even in the diner's merciless overhead lighting.

"Talk me through this," Ruby said, stirring her coffee, which was strong enough to make editorial decisions. "How do I not completely humiliate myself?"

"Honesty." Luna pointed her fork at Ruby for emphasis, a piece of pancake threatening to fly. "That's the whole thing. People can tell when someone's phoning it in. But when it's real? When the performer is actually feeling it? The audience locks in."

"What if they don't get it? What if they want Dolly?"

"Some of them will want Dolly. And that's fine. The Dolly isn't going anywhere. This is about range. Adding dimension." Luna took a bite of her pancakes, chewed thoughtfully. "Tell me about Loretta. Why her?"

Ruby thought about it. She'd been thinking about it for weeks, really, turning it over like a stone in her pocket. "Because she's real. She doesn't sugarcoat. She talks about poverty, domestic violence, women's rights. She makes country music that's actually about something."

"And?"

"And because my grandmother loved her. Played her records every Sunday while she cleaned. I grew up hearing that voice in the kitchen, the living room, everywhere. Loretta was... she was the one white woman my grandmother fully trusted." Ruby smiled at the absurdity of it. "She'd say, 'Loretta knows what work is. Loretta knows what tired is.' Like that was the highest compliment she could give."

"There it is." Luna set down her fork. "That's the connection. Not an impersonation. A conversation across time. Between Loretta and Mabel and Darius and Ruby and everyone who ever worked themselves down to nothing and kept singing anyway."

"That's a lot of pressure for a Wednesday night in Midtown."

"All the best art happens under weird pressure. That's how diamonds work. Or yogurt. One of the two."

At the table next to them, a woman was telling an elaborate story about a wedding in Buckhead where the bride's Louboutin heels had turned out to be counterfeits, the signature red soles flaking off with every step down the aisle, leaving a trail of red specks in the grass like some kind of budget fairy tale. Her friends were in hysterics. The bride, apparently, had kept walking like absolutely nothing was happening, which the storyteller considered "the most iconic thing I have ever personally witnessed with my own eyes."

Ruby listened and felt something settle. Sometimes the coating came off. Sometimes the thing underneath wasn't what anyone expected. The question was whether a person kept walking.

"I'm scared," Ruby said. "Not just of bombing. Of what it means. A Black queen doing Loretta Lynn. People are going to have opinions."

Luna looked at her steadily. "People have opinions about everything. People have opinions about whether water is wet. The question isn't whether someone has an opinion. The question is whether the art is honest." She leaned forward. "Is it honest?"

"It's the most honest thing I've ever wanted to do."

"Then do it. And let the opinions catch up."

The Cabaret on a Wednesday night was a different animal than Friday. The crowd was smaller, maybe sixty people instead of a hundred and fifty, and the energy was quieter, more intimate, less performative. The bachelorette parties were absent. The birthday groups were home. What remained were the regulars, the devotees, the people who came to The Cabaret because they loved drag, not because it was a novelty.

Bo had promoted the new act with characteristic understatement: a single Instagram post that read, "Ruby Ridges. New material. Wednesday. Don't miss it." She'd added a fire emoji, which for Bo was the equivalent of a full-page newspaper ad.

The club smelled the way it always did: beer and cologne and the particular sweetness of fog machine fluid, with an undertone of the carpet's ancient mysteries. The framed photos on the walls watched from their smudged glass, decades of performers bearing witness. The lighting rig hummed overhead, and Ruby could see the gaffer tape holding one of the gel filters in place, a detail that had never bothered her before but that now felt like a metaphor she didn't want to examine too closely.

Luna Tick was in the front row, wearing a silver dress that caught every available photon of light, grinning with the barely contained energy of someone who knew a secret. Beside her sat Jerome and his boyfriend, Cole, who

111

came every Friday and had apparently rearranged their schedule for a Wednesday. A few tables back, Ruby spotted Tasha and Dominique from the Saturday cast, which meant word had gotten around. Bo stood at her usual post by the sound board, arms crossed, face unreadable.

Ruby waited backstage, wearing the prairie dress, her hands shaking so badly she'd had to redo her lipstick twice. The makeup was different tonight. Simpler. Less Dolly's exaggerated glamour, more Loretta's understated beauty. She'd kept her own eyebrows, darkened them, let her face be closer to itself than it had been onstage in fifteen years.

The emcee, a queen named Pepper LaBeija who'd been hosting Wednesdays since forever, leaned into the microphone. "Alright, babies. We have something different tonight. Fifteen years of Dolly, and our girl Ruby Ridges is trying on a whole new woman. Be kind, be present, and for the love of God, put the phones away for five minutes. Ruby?"

Ruby walked out.

The stage lights hit her, and for a moment she couldn't see anything beyond the glare. Then her eyes adjusted, and there was the room, smaller than Friday, more intimate, faces she could actually distinguish. Luna Tick's silver dress blazing in the front row. Jerome leaning forward, phone already up. The woman at the corner table with her hand on her girlfriend's knee.

The crowd went quiet. Ruby could feel them taking in the dress, the different makeup, the absence of rhinestones and sequins and everything they associated with Ruby Ridges. She looked, she knew, like someone they hadn't met yet.

The opening notes of "Coal Miner's Daughter" started. Sparse. Acoustic guitar and the ghost of a melody. Just the simplest bones of a song.

Ruby opened her mouth, and her voice cracked on the first note.

The silence that followed was the worst three seconds of her life. She could feel the audience holding its breath, could feel the collective clench of sixty people who didn't know whether this was part of the act or a genuine disaster. Luna's smile had frozen. Bo uncrossed her arms.

"Well," Ruby said into the microphone, her voice steadier than she felt, "turns out being terrified makes a person forget how to sing. My grandmother would have had something to say about that. Probably 'Stop showing out and just open your mouth, child.'"

The laughter came, warm and relieved, and something in the room released.

Ruby started again.

This time the voice came from somewhere deeper, somewhere she hadn't accessed onstage before. It wasn't Dolly's bright soprano. It wasn't even Loretta's mezzo, not exactly. It was something in between, something that belonged to Ruby and to Mabel and to every woman who'd ever sung along to the radio while doing work that nobody thanked her for. She sang about Butcher Hollow and growing up poor and being proud anyway, and as she sang, she felt the dress move with her, the cotton soft and forgiving, shifting like water, like memory.

She forgot a lyric in the second verse. Stopped. Laughed at herself, and the laugh was real, not a performance, just a person standing in a wedding dress on a Wednesday night, getting it wrong.

"Sorry, y'all. Give me a second. This is harder than it looks. Dolly never let me forget a lyric. Loretta, apparently, is less forgiving."

She started the verse again, and this time she nailed it, and she could feel the shift in the room, the moment the audience stopped watching a performance and started witnessing something. The woman at the corner table wiped her eyes. A man at the bar put his drink down and didn't pick it up again.

Between songs, Ruby talked. She talked about Mabel Ridges. About the turntable that skipped. About a woman who cleaned houses for families that would never invite her to dinner and came home too tired to eat but still braided her grandchild's hair and played Loretta Lynn records and said, "That woman knows." About learning, years later, that what Loretta knew and what Mabel knew were the same thing: that survival was not glamorous and that singing about it honestly was its own kind of resistance.

"People ask me sometimes why I do country," Ruby said, and she could feel the room tense slightly, the way rooms do when a Black performer names the thing everyone is thinking. "They mean, why does a Black queen from Georgia do white country music. And the answer is, it was never white to me. It was my grandmother's music. It was Sunday music. It was the sound of being loved by someone who was too tired for everything except love."

The silence that followed was a different kind of silence than the one after her voice cracked. This one had weight. This one had recognition.

She performed "Don't Come Home A-Drinkin' (With Lovin' on Your Mind)" and watched people sit forward, actually leaning toward the stage, their bodies making the decision before their minds caught up. The dress swirled as she moved, cream cotton catching the stage lights, and Ruby felt something she hadn't felt in years: the electric, terrifying, irreplaceable sensation of not knowing what was going to happen next.

She closed with "Coal Miner's Daughter" again, the full version this time, no cracks, no restarts, just the song and the dress and fifteen years of playing it safe burning away under the lights.

When she finished, the room was still.

One second. Two. Long enough for Ruby to think, with perfect clarity: I have made a terrible mistake.

Then Luna stood up. Mascara was running down her cheeks in dark rivers, and she was clapping so hard that Ruby could hear each individual impact, sharp and bright.

Jerome stood next. Then Cole. Then the woman at the corner table, still crying, pulling her girlfriend up with her. The applause built the way real applause builds, not all at once, not in unison, but in waves, one table and then another and then another, until the whole room was standing, and someone near the bar yelled "More!" and someone else picked it up.

Not everyone was crying. A couple at a back table clapped politely, the kind of applause that means "this was fine." A man near the door had his arms folded, his expression somewhere between confused and impressed. That was okay. That was real. Not every room converts completely. Not every risk pays off for every person in the audience.

But most of them were standing. Most of them were making noise. And Ruby, in her forty-two-dollar dress, bowed and felt something crack open in her chest that she'd been holding shut for fifteen years.

"Thank y'all," she said, her voice thick. "I only prepared the one act, so that's all there is tonight. But I'll be back next Wednesday. And the Wednesday after that. And I promise I'll know all the words by then."

The crowd laughed and kept clapping, and Ruby walked offstage on legs that barely held.

Backstage, she sat in front of her mirror, still in the dress, her reflection showing someone she was only beginning to recognize. The makeup was smudged from crying. The wig was slightly crooked. The lace panels at the sleeves had a small tear she hadn't noticed before, probably caught on the microphone stand.

She looked imperfect. She looked like herself.

There was a knock on the dressing room door.

"Come in."

Luna Tick entered, mascara destroyed, foundation streaked, looking like a beautiful painting left out in the rain. She didn't say anything for a moment. She just stood there, and then she sat down next to Ruby, their shoulders touching, and they looked at their reflections together in the mirror ringed with flickering lights.

"That was the drag I've been waiting to see," Luna said quietly.

"I forgot a whole verse."

"Nobody cared."

"A couple people looked confused."

"A couple people look confused at everything. That's just their face." Luna paused. "Thank you. For being brave."

"Thank you for being annoying enough to make me try." Ruby nudged her. "And for being twenty-one and thinking that gives a person the right to have opinions about everything."

"It absolutely does give me that right."

"It does not."

"Agree to disagree."

They sat together, drag mother and drag daughter, looking at their reflections. The mirror had seen fifteen years of Ruby's transformations. Tonight's was different from all the others.

"So," Luna said. "Next week?"

Ruby thought about it. The fear was still there. It would probably always be there, and maybe that was the point, maybe the fear was what made it mean something. "Maybe Etta James. Or Nina Simone. Something that scares me."

"And maybe a TikTok collab? Just one dance. Thirty seconds. The algorithm would lose its mind."

"Absolutely not."

"The algorithm, Ruby."

"No."

"Three weeks," Luna said, holding up three fingers with the absolute certainty of someone who had never once been told no in a way that stuck. "Give me three weeks."

Bo appeared in the doorway, leaning against the frame, arms crossed in her characteristic stance. Her expression was the same one she'd worn by the sound board, unreadable, assessing. Then the corner of her mouth twitched.

"Not bad, baby," she said. "Not bad at all."

"Wednesday crowd," Ruby said. "Easier room."

"Wednesday crowd is a harder room and everybody knows it. Those are the real ones. The ones who know when someone's faking." Bo straightened up. "Do that again next week. And the week after. We'll talk about the schedule in a month."

She left without saying more, because Bo had never been talented at more. But her hand brushed the doorframe on the way out, a gesture so small Ruby might have imagined it, a gentle tap, almost like a benediction.

Ruby drove home still wearing the prairie dress, windows down, Atlanta's humid night air rushing through the car. The city was lit up and alive around her, the skyline bright against the dark, and she was tired in the way that only real work makes a person tired, the good kind, the kind that means something was spent that needed spending.

In the rearview mirror, she caught a glimpse of herself: makeup smudged, wig slightly askew, cream-colored cotton dress wrinkled from three hours of wearing her heart onstage in a Midtown warehouse on a Wednesday night.

She didn't look like Dolly. She didn't look like Loretta.

She looked like Ruby Ridges, which, it turned out, had been the whole point all along.

Cleanup on Aisle 5

I have lived many lives. Seven, perhaps eight. Possibly nine if anyone counts the courthouse lunch hour in Oakland when the bride declared she wanted a marriage with less tradition and more snacks.

That wedding lasted forty-seven minutes, including the part where the groom's mother tried to object and the judge said, "Ma'am, this is a civil ceremony, not a soap opera."

I've survived a lot. Alterations by someone who clearly learned to sew from a YouTube video. A cousin who tried to step into me without unzipping anything, which resulted in sounds I can only describe as structural violence. Three different bachelorette parties where I was used as a photo prop and somehow ended up covered in glitter that I'm still finding in my seams. A reception where the bride's uncle decided to demonstrate the Charleston and took out an entire champagne tower.

My shape is simple. Classic that doesn't need to announce itself because it knows what it's doing. Sleeveless with a sweetheart neckline that flatters without making promises it can't keep. A gentle A-line skirt that glides when you walk and doesn't require a team of engineers to sit down in. A quiet slit along my right leg, visible only when movement insists on honesty.

My bodice carries rhinestones arranged with the half-precise, half-chaotic energy of David's Bridal merchandise from 2003. I know exactly what I am. I'm not ashamed.

My color is burnt orange ombre, fading from a deep sunset at the waist into a warm sherbet glow at the hem. I've been called tangerine dream, creamsicle formal, and "that orange situation" by a woman who ultimately bought me anyway and wore me to her daughter's wedding with a defiant joy that made me proud.

Miss Yolanda once said the shade reminded her of a sky she saw on Martha's Vineyard, which she claimed was the prettiest place she had ever stood in real life. I tucked that compliment into my seams like a blessing and have been dining out on it ever since.

I am proud of who I am. I have earned my pride through sheer survival.

Now I live in a thrift store in Bakersfield, California, where lights flatten everyone's ego eventually and the air conditioning fights a losing battle against the dry heat pressing through inadequate insulation. This is where hopes come to rest or reinvent themselves. It depends on the person. And the fabric.

I hang between a yellow prom dress and a mother-of-the-bride suit. They do not speak, but I can feel their opinions as clearly as breath.

The prom dress vibrates with the delusional belief that she was meant for a Macy's window, eternally caught mid-twirl, despite the fact that her hem has been duct-taped twice and she smells faintly of Axe body spray. The mother-of-the-bride suit holds her dignity so tightly her shoulder pads

119

have developed their own structural integrity. Her lining is heavy with gospel memories and the specific righteousness of someone who has seen the congregation through four pastors and is not impressed with any of them.

A leather jacket two racks down radiates the smug satisfaction of someone who once belonged to a man who definitely owned a motorcycle, possibly a warrant, and absolutely no business dating anyone's daughter. That jacket has seen things. It judges me for my rhinestones.

We all have stories. Some of us simply embroider them with more confidence.

Customers drift through our aisle like thunderstorms that cannot decide on a direction. Last week, a college girl pressed me against her body, declared me "almost perfect," and then announced she would cut me into a club top.

A club top.

My hanger trembled with the weight of my offense.

She bought a sequined shrug instead, and I exhaled in relief.

Another customer tried to drape me over her dog. The dog was a Chihuahua named Precious who looked personally victimized by the entire experience. I refused to cooperate. The woman left muttering about "difficult fabrics" as if I were the problem in that situation.

But this morning, something altogether different arrived.

It began with urgency. The kind that cannot be reasoned with.

The morning fog pressed low over Bakersfield, turning the air heavy and wet like a towel that never quite dried. The store felt cold enough to make my skirt stiffen slightly, my ombre darkening in the dim light. I was contemplating my existence, as one does on slow Tuesday mornings, when the front door flew open with the violence of someone who had run out of options.

A woman stumbled in.

Not walked. Not entered. Stumbled.

She had the unmistakable posture of someone searching not for beauty, not for bargains, but for salvation in the form of a restroom.

"Oh no no no," she muttered, one hand clutching her stomach, the other braced against a rack of winter coats that had no business being out in August.

She wore scrubs. Faded blue with cartoon bears on them, the kind pediatric nurses wear to make sick children feel less scared. The scrubs were wrinkled like she'd slept in them, or more likely, like she hadn't slept at all. Her name tag dangled sideways, the name obscured by what looked like dried coffee or possibly evidence.

Her steps wobbled. Her breathing hitched. She looked around the store with the wild hope of someone who believes in miracles because she has no other choice.

She saw no restroom. Only racks of clothes and a sign at the register that read, in Miss Yolanda's careful handwriting, "No Public Bathrooms. Please Do Not Ask. Yes, We Mean It. No, Not Even For Emergencies. We're Sorry."

The woman whispered one small, panicked word the way people whisper prayers they don't expect God to answer.

"Please."

She jogged, which is a generous term for the lurching half-run of someone whose body was staging a very aggressive coup, toward the dressing rooms. She tugged at door after door. Locked. Occupied. Locked. Occupied.

One dressing room occupant said, "Someone's in here," with the tone of someone who believed emergencies belonged to other people and should have the decency to occur elsewhere.

The woman pressed her palm to her abdomen and bent forward, breathing in short, desperate bursts that sounded like a freight train approaching a tunnel.

"I just need a minute," she whispered.

But she did not have a minute left.

Her body had other plans, and those plans were immediate.

She staggered down my aisle, gripping racks for balance, weaving through forgotten gowns like a drunk person navigating a familiar room in the dark. Then she slipped behind me, dropping into the dim space between my skirt and the wall as if the soft chaos of thrift store fabric could save her.

Her forehead touched the linoleum. Cold. Industrial. Unforgiving.

She whispered something that sounded like bad choices wrapped in desperation and possibly a prayer to a God she wasn't sure was listening.

Miss Yolanda noticed her immediately. Miss Yolanda always notices things.

She's worked this floor for sixteen years, raised three kids on thrift store wages and church bake sales, and buried a husband who left her with a mortgage and a 1987 Buick that ran on faith and transmission fluid. She moves through these aisles like someone who understands that every person walking through that door is fighting something, and judgment is a luxury she can't afford.

Her eyes were warm but weary in that way only retail workers and healers understand. She approached carefully, her steps slow and steady, the way she'd approach a spooked animal or a crying child.

"Ma'am," she said gently. "Are you looking for something?"

The woman shook her head rapidly, her whole body trembling in protest.

"No bathrooms," Miss Yolanda said softly. "I am so sorry. There's a McDonald's two blocks down..."

The woman's breath hitched. Her shoulders curled inward. Her voice cracked like old china.

"I cannot... I cannot hold it."

She lurched forward.

And vomited.

On me.

Right on my burnt orange ombre skirt, the part that fades from sunset to sherbet, the part Miss Yolanda said looked like Martha's Vineyard.

The warmth hit first, soaking through my outer layer into the lining beneath, seeping into the tulle and the interfacing and every carefully constructed layer that had held me together through seven or eight or possibly nine weddings. Then the smell, sharp and sour, coffee and something sweet gone wrong, the specific horror of a body rejecting what it cannot process. Bile and what might have been a gas station breakfast burrito making a violent reappearance.

Then the sound.

Oh, the sound.

A wet surrender, intimate and awful, like a secret told to the wrong witness. The splatter, the heave, the gasping aftermath of a body that had reached its absolute limit and decided to make it everyone's problem.

Rhinestones do not deserve this level of betrayal.

The prom dress vibrated with horror so intense I thought she might faint. The mother-of-the-bride suit radiated silent prayer, probably Psalm 23, definitely including the part about walking through the valley of the shadow of death. The leather jacket pulsed with judgment so smug I wanted to set it on fire.

My skirt wilted beneath the flood of sour panic, trapped ache, poor decisions, and what I was now certain was definitely a gas station burrito.

Even for a dress who had seen things, this was a lot.

The woman blinked at the stain spreading across my hem, shame rising like tidewater, unstoppable and cold.

"I am so sorry," she whispered, but apologies cannot rewind moments like this. Apologies cannot unvomit a burrito.

Miss Yolanda stepped back first, startled by the violence of it, then forward again with the fierce tenderness that comes from years of cleaning up after people who cannot clean up after themselves.

"Honey," she said softly, pulling a pack of tissues from her pocket like she'd been preparing for exactly this moment her entire life. "You need air."

The woman tried to stand. Her legs disagreed. She grabbed my hem for support.

I felt the additional weight of her desperation and thought, This is it. This is how I die. Vomit-soaked in Bakersfield, California.

A customer at the end of the aisle stopped and stared. She who wore athleisure to go shopping and had opinions about other people's life choices. Her disgust arrived before her words, settling over the scene like nuclear fallout.

"Unbelievable," the customer said, her voice sharp enough to cut glass. "Some people make everything harder for everyone else."

The woman in scrubs lifted her head, bracing for cruelty, her face pale and slick with sweat.

"You don't even know me."

"I know what I'm seeing," the customer replied, crossing her arms like she was judge, jury, and the comment section of a news article.

It was not the worst insult in the world. But it carried the sting of someone who had never crouched behind a rack of dresses hoping life would give her one more chance. Someone who had never worked a double shift and driven home on fumes and prayers. Someone whose body had never betrayed her in public.

Miss Yolanda placed herself between them before words could sharpen further. She was small, Miss Yolanda, barely five foot two, but she had the presence of someone who had stared down worse things than a woman in athleisure with opinions.

"She's having a medical emergency," Miss Yolanda said quietly. "And unless you're planning to help, you can keep shopping or you can leave."

The athleisure woman's mouth opened, then closed. She grabbed a handbag she'd been considering and marched to the register with the rigid spine of someone who would definitely be leaving a Google review.

Miss Yolanda helped the woman in scrubs to her feet, one hand under her elbow, the other supporting her back.

"Come on, honey," she said. "Let's get you outside."

The woman stumbled toward the door, Miss Yolanda guiding her gently, and I watched through my haze of vomit and shame as they stepped into the heavy California air.

Through the front window, I could see them. Miss Yolanda handed the woman a bottle of water from her own bag. The woman drank it in desperate gulps, then leaned against the brick wall, crying quietly, one hand on her stomach, the other holding a phone she couldn't quite bring herself to answer.

It buzzed. And buzzed. And buzzed.

Finally, she answered it.

"Mom," she said, her voice breaking. "I can't... I can't do this anymore. I worked sixteen hours, I haven't slept, I can't keep anything down, and I just threw up in a thrift store."

I couldn't hear the other side of the conversation, but I saw the woman's face crumple and rebuild itself several times.

"I know," she said. "I know you need the money. But I need to sleep. I need to eat something that isn't from a vending machine. I need..." Her voice broke completely. "I need help."

She listened for a long moment, then nodded.

"Okay," she whispered. "Okay. I'm coming home."

She hung up. Stood there for another minute. Then walked away, steadier than she'd arrived, as if purging wasn't just physical.

Miss Yolanda watched her go, then turned back toward the store, her face set in the expression of someone about to deal with a very unpleasant situation.

She found me exactly where I'd been left. Soaked. Stained. Smelling like consequences.

The bell above the door chimed as she reentered, thin and sorrowful.

Inside, silence pooled around the racks like flood water.

Miss Yolanda returned to me slowly, kneeling in front of my stained skirt the way one kneels in front of a broken thing that still deserves tenderness.

She lifted my fabric between careful fingers, studying the damage. Coffee. Bile. The unmistakable evidence of a burrito that should have stayed theoretical.

"Oh honey," she whispered. "You did not deserve this."

Her voice wrapped around me like comfort, and for the first time since the warmth hit, I felt something other than disgust.

She carried me to the back room, laid me on the long table under the LED lights that made everything look worse than it was, and studied me with the expression of a surgeon assessing a patient who probably wouldn't make it.

She tried soap first. Cold water on a clean rag, dabbing gently at the edges of the stain. The smell retreated slightly, then returned with reinforcements.

Hot water next. A spray bottle of something that smelled like false promises and industrial lemons. She scrubbed gently, then harder, then gently again because she understood the difference between cleaning and destroying.

Nothing worked.

"Come on, sweetheart," she murmured, trying vinegar mixed with baking soda. The fizzing felt hopeful for a moment, like maybe chemistry could undo what the morning had done.

The stain faded at the edges. The center held its ground.

She tried dish soap. She tried club soda from the mini-fridge in the break room, the one marked "FRAN'S. DO NOT TOUCH. YES THAT MEANS YOU, SHANNA." She tried a paste made of something from under the sink that she'd been saving for true emergencies.

The stain had settled into my fibers with the permanence of a decision that couldn't be unmade. My burnt orange ombre now featured a new shade: regret and a hint of gas station protein.

Miss Yolanda sat back on her heels with a sigh that carries the weight of sixteen years in retail and all the things she couldn't fix.

The prom dress, visible through the doorway, vibrated with gossip she would definitely be sharing with the other formals. The mother-of-the-bride suit radiated empathy so pure it almost hurt. The leather jacket muttered internal condolences that sounded suspiciously like "I told you so."

"I'm sorry," Miss Yolanda said softly, and I realized she was talking to me. Not at me. To me. Like she knew I could hear. Like she understood that fabric holds more than thread.

"This is too much, sweetheart. I can't sell you like this. I can't even donate you like this."

She lifted me carefully, like someone lifting a memory she wished she could keep, and carried me to the large gray bin in the corner.

The unsellable bin. The last stop. The place where damaged things went to wait for whatever came next.

But before she lowered me in, she paused.

"You know," she said, smoothing my fabric one last time, "my grand-mother used to say that everything that comes through a thrift store is just passing through on its way to somewhere else. Nothing really ends here. It just... pauses. Waits for the right person to come along."

She folded me gently, arranging my skirt so the stain faced down, hidden.

"Maybe someone will come who sees past this. Someone who knows how to work with what's broken instead of throwing it away. There's people like that out there. Seamstresses with magic hands. Artists who see potential instead of problems." She smiled, though her eyes were tired. "I've seen dresses leave this store in worse shape than you and end up somewhere beautiful."

She lowered me into the bin.

"Rest now," she said. "Your story's not over. It's just waiting for its next chapter."

The lid closed with a soft click.

Not a period. An ellipsis.

Darkness folded around me. My fabric cooled. My rhinestones dimmed. The smell lingered.

I could still hear the store breathing. Hangers scraping. The register chiming. Miss Yolanda's voice helping another customer find their size. Life continuing without ceremony.

I have been here before. Not this bin, not this smell, but this moment. The pause between what was and whatever comes next.

I remember the bride in Sacramento who laughed so hard she cried into my bodice when the flower girl sneezed seventeen times during the ceremony. I remember the courthouse wedding in Oakland where the groom's hands shook and the bride said, "We have time," and meant it. I remember the VFW hall where someone's abuela danced with me after the bride kicked off her shoes, spinning me like I belonged to her.

I remember joy. I remember grief. I remember the weight of both.

And I remember her.

The woman in scrubs. The apology she whispered. The moment her body refused one more act of endurance. The phone call she finally answered. The help she finally asked for.

Dresses do not judge. We hold.

Fabric remembers what bodies cannot carry forever.

Miss Yolanda thought she should send it to "that woman in Carson who fixes the unfixable." She's someone who sees past damage. Someone who knows how to work with what's been broken instead of throwing it away. People like that exist. I've known them. I've been reshaped by them.

Or maybe no one comes.

128

Maybe I stay here in the dark, rhinestones dulling, ombre fading, my story paused indefinitely.

Even so, I have done my work.

I held someone when they fell apart. I carried what they couldn't.

That is not nothing.

That is holy.

The lid stays closed. The story waits.

.

The Inheritance

The first time my aunt tried to leave me something in a will, it was a bread machine.

The second time, it was a cursed wedding dress.

At least the bread machine had instructions.

Mr. Mensah, our family lawyer, adjusted his glasses and read in his gentle accountant voice, "To my beloved niece Sophia, my beloved nephew Oliver, my beloved grandniece Madison, and whoever else my brother dragged in here out of guilt, I leave the following: nothing. Yet."

Oliver stiffened. Madison, who had already angled her phone to get "tasteful mournful lighting," froze mid-tilt. I stopped mentally counting how many condolence casseroles were in my fridge.

Mr. Mensah cleared his throat. "She continues. 'Nothing, yet, because you people never listen all the way through.'" He looked up at us over the paper. "Her words. Not mine."

Of course they were. Aunt Martha had been dramatically herself right up until the part where her heart forgot to keep beating on a Wednesday.

Mr. Mensah lifted another sheet of paper. "Item one. The dress."

He said it with capital letters. The Dress.

Oliver frowned. "What dress?"

Madison's eyes lit up. "Please let this involve a reality show."

Mr. Mensah smiled faintly. "Your aunt writes: 'You remember the dress. If you do not, I have failed you more deeply than I feared.'"

I did remember.

I remembered the way it swallowed an entire closet by itself, a polyester hurricane contained by wire hangers and wishful thinking. The way ten-year-old me had dragged it out, climbed into the skirt, and disappeared up to my chin in a sea of tulle and ambition. I remembered the faint smell of old perfume and stress sweat when she showed it to me, rolling her eyes and calling it "The Monument to My Worst Decision and Best Escape."

The dress had been the first and only thing she ever bought on credit. A wedding gown that looked like it had lost a bet with the seventies: shiny satin, sleeves like hostile balloons, lace that scratched your skin if you breathed too deeply. She never wore it down an aisle. The wedding never happened.

Mr. Mensah kept reading. "Your aunt writes: 'My wedding dress is currently hanging on the bridal rack at Eco Thrift. It is the one that looks like a frosted victim and has inexplicable blue beads in the hem.'"

I blinked. "She donated it?"

"She donated almost everything," Mr. Mensah said. "House, furniture, clothes. She wanted her life to be picked up one piece at a time instead of boxed up and thrown out in bulk. Her phrase."

That was aggressively on brand.

He lifted the final page. "To continue. 'Whichever of you can follow the clues in that dress and explain what it truly meant to me will inherit the rest of my estate. The dress knows. Follow its clues. If none of you manage, the money goes to Eco Thrift to fix their roof before Fran falls through it.'"

"Who is Fran," Oliver demanded.

"Volunteer," I said automatically. "Yellow visor, bingo champion, possibly immortal."

"Wait." Madison leaned forward. "When she says 'the rest of my estate,' how much are we talking? Like car money, or delete-your-student-loans-and-buy-a-boat money?"

Mr. Mensah shuffled his papers with the careful precision of someone who'd rehearsed this moment. "Between the investment account, the unspent pension, the house sale, and a surprisingly valuable collection of vintage Pyrex, your aunt left roughly one point six million dollars."

The air in the conference room changed.

One point six million dollars is enough to make your brother's eye twitch in a whole new rhythm. Enough to make time slow down and speed up simultaneously. Enough to turn oxygen into something you had to remember to process manually.

"It is not a prank," Mr. Mensah added, before Oliver could start. "I have verified the accounts."

Madison's phone was suddenly in her purse, vanished like a magic trick performed by someone who'd just realized this was serious. "Okay, so, thrift store heist. When do we start?"

I rubbed my temples. The lights buzzed overhead like judgmental insects placing bets on our inevitable dysfunction. Aunt Martha, who once left a note on my car that said "Your tire looks sad, I added some air, you are welcome," had orchestrated an inheritance scavenger hunt.

Of course she had.

"The will gives you seven days," Mr. Mensah said. "You must begin at the dress. Everything else follows."

Oliver pushed back his chair with the decisive scrape of someone who'd just spotted a problem that could be solved with a sufficiently detailed spreadsheet. "Fantastic. We will go right now."

"We will?" I said.

He gave me the look he reserves for people who do not update their LinkedIn regularly. Oliver liked to present his life in bullet points. Senior financial analyst. Marathon finisher. Man who absolutely does not need one point six million dollars, but would still like to win on principle because winning proves you were paying attention.

"Sophia," he said, "this is what she wanted. For us to engage, process, honor her memory."

Madison made a sound halfway between a laugh and a scoff. "He means compete for cash, confess on camera, sabotage each other, and eventually reveal long buried secrets while someone plays emotional piano music."

We both stared at her.

"What," she said. "That is literally the plot of every show I watch. I have waited my whole life for this narrative arc."

Mr. Mensah folded the will with hands that moved like he was tucking a child into bed. "One warning. Your aunt added a final note at the bottom, in pen. 'Do not turn this into cheap drama. I can feel you trying from beyond the grave and I am not impressed. Remember, the dress is not a game piece. It is a witness.'"

I felt that line settle somewhere under my ribs where anxiety liked to build vacation homes.

A witness. Not a prize.

Oliver was already halfway to the door, car keys jingling like tiny bells announcing the start of a race no one had agreed to run.

"First one to the thrift store gets the first clue," he called.

"That is not how clues work," I muttered, but I followed anyway.

It is hard to resist a mystery when the detective is your dead aunt and the reward is enough money to buy back every bad decision you ever financed on a credit card. Also, I really wanted to see who, exactly, had thought that dress was bridal material.

All the dress discovery, curtains, dresser, safety deposit box, notebook sections stay exactly as written]

I opened the envelope with hands that shook slightly.

Inside was a check. Made out to "Eco Thrift Community Fund." Signed by my aunt in her looping script. For one hundred thousand dollars.

Underneath the check, a Post-it note in purple ink: "For the roof before Fran falls through it, the raise Darius will not ask for because he is too good for this world, Fran's knee surgery because she refuses to admit she needs it, and maybe fix that bathroom door that does not lock. Also get Gerald the squirrel a friend. He looks lonely."

Under that, another Post-it: "No, this is not the inheritance, do not get comfortable. I am not that predictable. Keep going. You are doing great. Have you been drinking water? Drink some water."

Oliver exhaled through his nose like a pressure valve releasing steam. "She really made us do side quests. There are literally side quests in this inheritance."

"Be grateful," Madison said. "We are leveling up our emotional intelligence stats. This is character development. This is growth."

I picked up the spiral notebook. On the front, in silver marker, Martha had written: "WRITE WHAT YOU THINK THIS DRESS IS ABOUT BEFORE YOU READ ANYTHING ELSE. NO CHEATING. YES, OLIVER, I MEAN YOU."

"Sophia," she wrote, and I felt my name like a hand on my shoulder. "If I leave you one point six million dollars, you will panic. You will immediately feel responsible for everyone within a fifty-mile radius who has ever experienced a minor inconvenience. You will google 'how to give away money without being weird about it' and then feel guilty about the electricity you used to google it.

"You will also probably think the money is the answer. That having resources will finally make you capable of fixing things, of being useful, of mattering.

"But here is what I need you to understand: You have always been useful. You have always mattered. The money is not permission to start helping people. It is just permission to help more people the way you already help.

"The money is not the inheritance, sweetheart. The mindset is.

"You will also sit down at a table, probably this table, in this thrift store, with Darius and Fran and whoever else wanders over because they heard there was coffee, and you will ask, quietly and seriously, 'Okay. What do we fix first?' You will not make a show of it. You will not turn it into content. You will not need applause.

"You will just do it. The way you have always done it, in small ways nobody noticed. Refilling soap dispensers. Checking in on people. Remembering birthdays. Sending the thoughtful text. Showing up when it is boring.

"That is why I am leaving it to you. Not because you will spend the money correctly. But because you already understand that money does not fix people. Presence does. Maintenance does. The unglamorous work of showing up again and again does.

"The money just means you can afford to show up in more places."

The room went very quiet.

I stared at the words. At the part where she said I had always been useful. At the part where the money was described not as the solution, but as a tool I had already earned the right to use.

Somewhere on the third floor, Stevie Nicks was singing about landslides and getting older. Someone's phone buzzed. A customer dropped a snow globe and it did not break, just rolled sadly across the floor until it bumped against my shoe.

135

"Because I trust you," Martha had written at the bottom of the page, "to remember the dress.

"And if you forget, it is okay. The dress remembers you."

"What do we do with it now?" I asked.

Darius grinned and handed me one last folded note from the bottom of the box.

"Please put the dress back on the rack," it read. "Price it at whatever you think a revelation is worth. Let someone else buy it and discover their own truths in the lining. But before you do, stitch one more thing into the hem. Not for me. For you. This is the real inheritance. Not the money. This."

I stared at the note, then at the dress in my mind's eye. At the blue beads for courage, the red stitch pointing toward hidden truths, the floral lining that used to be curtains in a house where she learned to choose herself.

What could I possibly add to that?

A small, ridiculous idea occurred to me.

"Do you have any beads?" I asked Darius.

"Do I have beads?" he repeated, offended on behalf of craft supplies everywhere. "This is a thrift store. We have beads that have outlived marriages. We have beads that predate the internet. We have beads that might be cursed. Take your pick."

He brought over a plastic tub from under the counter. Inside, a riot of colors and sizes tumbled together like a tiny treasure hoard.

I dug through them until my fingers found it. A small, plain wooden bead, sanded smooth from use or age or both. Nothing flashy. Nothing that would catch light or draw attention. The kind of bead that would blend into a hem so completely you would only find it if you were looking.

Or if you needed it.

I threaded a needle with hands that shook slightly.

We climbed back up to the third floor, to the bridal section.

At the edge of the hem, next to one of Martha's blue beads for courage, I carefully stitched my wooden bead in with a single line of thread.

"For what?" Madison asked softly.

"Maintenance," I said.

"Maintenance?" Oliver repeated, like I had just invented a new word.

I tied off the stitch. Snipped the thread with the tiny scissors Darius handed me. Held the hem in my lap like a prayer I had finally learned to say out loud.

"Courage is loud," I said, the words coming out slowly, carefully, like I was building something fragile and important out of sound. "Escape is dramatic. Choosing yourself is a revolution that gets talked about at dinner parties. But somebody has to stick around after the grand gesture. Somebody has to do laundry and fill out insurance paperwork and call the roofer about the leak and show up on Tuesday morning when nothing interesting is happening and the coffee is bad but you drink it anyway because being present matters more than being inspired."

I looked at the bead, almost invisible against the yellowed fabric.

"Somebody has to maintain the life you chose. That is the part I have always been terrified I would mess up. The boring part. The part nobody writes songs about or makes into movies. The part where you just... keep going. Keep showing up. Keep fixing small things before they become big things.

"Martha kept saying the dress is the inheritance. The dress, not the money. I think this is what she meant. The blue beads are courage to leave. The red thread is courage to look inside. And this..." I touched the wooden bead gently. "This is courage to stay. To maintain. To show up. The money is just a tool. This is the lesson."

I held the dress up to the light. The hem caught the bright glow. Blue beads glittered like tiny promises Martha had made to herself. The red thread glowed like a path leading home from wherever you had gotten lost.

And my wooden bead, plain, unremarkable, true, disappeared into the fabric like it had been there all along.

Waiting.

Darius pressed both hands to his heart with the dramatic flair of someone who had just witnessed something holy happening in the bridal section of a thrift store. "If you do not stop, I am going to cry into the vintage handbags on the second floor and ruin them with my feelings."

Fran pulled a tissue from somewhere inside her visor. "Too late. I am already gone. Someone help me. I am emotionally compromised."

Madison reached over and squeezed my hand. She did not pull out her phone. Did not angle for the light. Did not perform the moment for an audience that was not here.

Just squeezed.

And when I looked at her, her eyes were wet and her smile was real and she looked like someone I remembered from before she learned to commodify vulnerability.

"That is really good, Sophia," she said quietly. "That is exactly right. That is the bead I did not know we needed. And honestly? That is the inheritance none of us knew we needed."

Oliver cleared his throat roughly. "For the record," he said, his voice doing something complicated, "I would have messed this up. I would have turned it into a project with phases and benchmarks. You are going to do better."

"I am going to mess it up differently," I said. "But thank you."

I stepped out into the afternoon light, the bell jangling behind me like applause.

One point six million dollars was a significant amount of money. But as I stood there in the parking lot, watching Oliver and Madison argue good-naturedly about where to get lunch, I realized Martha was right.

The money was not the answer. The money had never been the answer.

I had been showing up for people my whole life. Checking in. Remembering. Maintaining. Doing the unglamorous work of being present when it was boring, when there was no applause, when nobody was watching.

The money just meant I could afford to do more of what I had always done.

Patch a roof before someone fell through it. Fund scholarships for kids who needed permission to want things. Give Darius the raise he would never ask for. Pay for Fran's knee surgery. Fix that damn bathroom door. Commission a friend for Gerald so he would not have to spend eternity alone, frozen mid-leap, wearing sunglasses.

Small things. Maintenance things. The kind of kindnesses that do not get headlines but make it possible to keep going when the grand gestures have faded and you are just trying to make it to Thursday.

The wooden bead was the inheritance.

The money was just the means.

"Okay," I said, to the dress still hanging on the third floor, to my aunt wherever she was probably laughing at us, to the massive thrift store and Gerald and whoever might find a wooden bead in a hem someday and wonder what it meant.

"Let us see what we can fix first."

Three months later, I came back to Eco Thrift to drop off some chairs I had found at an estate sale. Good chairs. Solid. The kind that could hold weight without complaining.

The dress was gone.

In its place on the third-floor bridal rack hung a note on the empty hanger, written in Darius's handwriting.

"Sold to a woman who said she needed it for a wedding. Not her wedding. Her grandmother's second wedding. The grandmother is eighty-seven and marrying her girlfriend of forty years because they can finally legally do it and she wants to wear something that understands the wait. She looked inside. Found the beads. Cried. Said, 'This dress knows.' Paid asking price plus a hundred-dollar tip because she said the dress was undervalued. Fran cried. I cried. Gerald approved."

At the bottom, in purple ink that I recognized:

"P.S. She found your bead. Asked what it was for. I told her. She said, 'Good. Someone needs to say that out loud.' She is going to add her own before the wedding. The dress continues. Love, Darius."

I pressed the note to my chest and smiled.

The dress had moved on. Found someone else who needed it. Would keep accumulating stories and beads and stains and meaning until the fabric finally gave up or until the end of time, whichever came first.

Just like Martha wanted.

I walked back outside into the sunshine, got in my car (new used car, paid for in cash, air conditioning that worked), and drove to the nonprofit office I was setting up.

There was a roof to patch. A bathroom door to fix. Scholarships to fund. Small, unglamorous maintenance work that would never make headlines but would keep things running.

I was good at that. I had always been good at that.

The money just meant I could be good at it for more people.

But the real inheritance, the one that mattered, the one I would carry forward long after the bank account was empty?

That was already stitched into the hem of my life, invisible and essential, a plain wooden bead that taught me what Martha had known all along:

The dress knew.

And now, finally, so did I.

The End

Dr. Nandi Sojourner Crosby is an award-winning author, Black feminist sociologist, and professor whose work lives at the crossroads of justice, memory, humor, and radical tenderness. Her memoir, *Prisoners I Once Loved*, chronicles decades-long relationships with incarcerated women and men and has received wide acclaim for its emotional honesty.

A living kidney donor and TEDx speaker, Dr. Nandi has taught internationally and spent more than two decades as Professor of Sociology at California State University, Chico. When not writing or teaching, she can be found in thrift stores, lingering over objects with pasts insisting she was the original donor of the object, or at home in Northern California with her husband, cat, and hundreds of indoor plants.

Gently Used grew from her lifelong belief that secondhand stories matter, that humor and heartbreak belong together, and that the most honest versions of ourselves are stitched together imperfectly, with grace and a little magic.